The Fat Girls Club

A Novel

by

Lila Johnson

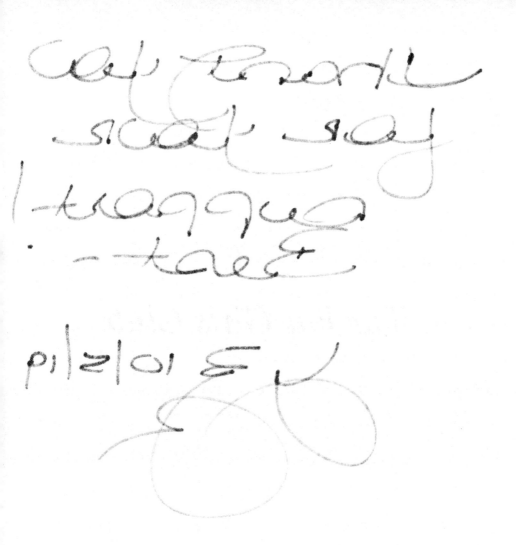

Cover Art: Maria Lis Cabriza - fineartamerica.com/profiles/maria-cabriza.html
Cover Design: Acclaim Graphics

ISBN: 0692317821
ISBN 13: 9780692317822

To Charli Coon

Thank you

✝ February 12, 2015

Acknowledgments

"Talent is cheaper than table salt. What separates the talented individual from the successful one is a lot of hard work."
- Stephen King

For many reasons, I am truly grateful:

First, I want to give all honor and glory to God. He has blessed me with a wonderful talent and placed many people in my path.

To my sister, Loretta, editor. I know it was hard for you to move past taking a nap or editing my work. Thanks for doing the latter.

To my father my who provided the shelter that helped me to write the words.

A big hug to Maria Lis Cabriza. You brought my characters to life with your skills as a visionary painter. What was once abstract in my mind, became real with the stroke of your paint brush!

To Flask Robins and Jeff Murphy, General Contractors. Your expertise in the world of construction enlightened my world and my story.

To Sheryl Armstrong-Hearns. Thank you for your insight and input as a design consultant.

To the group at Acclaim Graphics in Evansville, IN. You never left me hanging. Because of you, I was able to get the word out about my books through postcards that you helped to create. You are the best.

Thank you to all the Kansas City, Kansas and Kansas City, Missouri businesses and sites that are mentioned in this novel.

Finally I want to thank the many fans, friends, co-workers and believers of my first book.
Because you took a chance on me, it strengthens the belief I have in myself. Without you, I could not have moved forward with this, my second book. I will always be grateful.

"Everything you can imagine is real."- Pablo Picasso

one

et's get one thing straight. I'm fat. My name is Sissy Bakersfield
and I have a grudge. For those of you that stare me down in public
please don't call me a "big girl, pleasingly plump or full figured." I can
sum it up in two words for you: I'm fat.

Most women my size would try to cover up, lie or make a joke
about it. The plain and simple truth is that I gorged, pigged out and
fell in love with food because it loved me back with no questions asked.
I'm not the only one in this bind. Two of my friends are even larger
than I am and don't want to face the truth.

Angela Banks, whom I've known since kindergarten, is a size eighteen. Nicki Cole, my best friend since junior high school, wears a size
twenty-two. Believe it or not I'm the smallest at five-foot and wearing a
size fourteen or sixteen depending on the outfit.

It's so frustrating to sit back and watch the "thin" girls get the guys.
Don't get me wrong, a size three isn't necessary, but a ten would feel
and look so much better. I hate the feeling of being fat. And let's not
even discuss trying to climb a flight of stairs! Just running after a bus
could prove to be downright disastrous – if I should pass out, someone
might mistake me for a wounded cow and take me to the slaughter
house!

We are a *thick crew* in need of love and a good diet. I thought this
matter over while downing a raspberry iced tea and a large order of
tater tots at the Sonic drive-in. My gang and I need to get it together
and adopt a healthier lifestyle. Now, when I drop this health kick idea
on my girls, they'll have a fit. Angela will toss her weaved hair over her

shoulders and say that she is just fine. Nicki, on the other hand, may give it a try but will require a lot of hand holding.

Twelve-fifteen! – time to meet my girls at Cracker Barrel for lunch. I know they won't go for the idea of a weight loss program but I'm going to stand my ground, eat a corn muffin and tell them that a change is coming whether they like it or not. *The Fat Girls Club* is officially in session!

two

"What did you just call us," Angela said in a voice one octave higher than normal.

"The Fat Girls Club," Sissy repeated. Angela, aka "Miss Thing", rolled her eyes with those crazy butterfly lashes, turned and looked at Nicki while shaking her head.

"Stop it Angela," Sissy scolded. "If you could just be honest for once, you'd know that what I'm saying is true."

"I think it's kind of cute," Nicki chimed in. "I have to admit that I could stand to lose a few pounds but it's so hard. Besides, men like a woman with a little meat on her bones."

"A little meat, not half of a cow - and before you get upset, that last statement was meant for me," Sissy insisted.

Angela turned and pointed her finger, "Where do you get off telling us that we need to lose weight? I happen to like my pounds and the way I look. Besides, the men I date aren't ashamed to be seen with me. I love myself just the way I am thank you." She brushed at the auburn and gold highlighted weave of hair that cascaded over her shoulders.

"Look, I'm not trying to hurt anyone's feelings but it's time to get real."

"Oh, thank you Dr. Phil," she smirked.

Shaking her head at Angela's smart remark, Sissy continued. "We need to sit down and make a list of the pros and cons for losing weight and exercising. And while we're at it, we need to add reasons why we're not in a serious relationship."

3

The conversation paused while the waitress took orders. Nicki and Angela went for the same meal, *chicken fried chicken*; "I like this thicker cut of meat as opposed to the chicken fried steak," Angela explained. Nicki agreed while ordering potatoes with white gravy, corn, and green beans. Sissy ordered the grilled chicken strips over a bed of rice with carrots and cauliflower. As Sissy buttered a corn muffin Nicki spoke, "You know Angela, Sissy's right. Deep down inside, I have a desire to lose at least fifty pounds. I wouldn't admit this to anyone except the two of you but being a size twenty-two isn't fun. Remember that song by the Miracles, *The Tears of a Clown?*" The two women nodded. "That's me. Smiling on the outside but crying on the inside." She turned her head to the left and tried to discreetly wipe away a tear. Angela reached over and patted her hand. "See what you've started Sissy?" she said with a smirk on her lips.

"Stop Angela," Nicki hissed. "You're just mad because she opened the door to something we didn't want to face."

The food arrived, and after saying grace, all started eating without uttering a word. Finally, Sissy spoke. "Look, I'm not here to cause trouble or make anyone cry. I just wanted to tell you what I thought and felt."

"I understand that you care Sissy," Nicki said between a bite of chicken, "but what brought this on? We've been content with our lives and now you want to shake them up."

"Yeah," Angela started as she pointed her fork in Sissy's direction. "If you want to lose weight, that's cool, but don't bring that mess to the table and rock our world. Cody *loves* this big woman just as she is."

Sissy swatted at the mini pitch fork, but Angela moved it before she could knock it out of her hand. "OK, fine, sorry I brought the whole thing up. I thought it would be a fun way to tone up and lose a few pounds, nothing major. In addition, we'd feel better, look sexier and bounce through our day with so much more energy."

"You really need to stop reading so many *Prevention* and *Oprah* magazines. You're starting to sound like them." Angela stabbed at the last of her green beans and laughed at her own joke. Sissy shook her head then pushed the empty plate out of the way.

"Look ladies, I'm not going to give up on this, in fact, I've only just begun! Desert anyone?"

After throwing the keys on the hallway table, Sissy went straight to her bedroom and slowly removed her clothes stripping down to her underwear. For years she'd avoided the full length mirror inside her closet door. Over time she became clever at avoiding it but today was different. Today a truth would be told. She opened the door and stood in front of the mirror, her hands going immediately to her abdomen. Poking at the large pillow of flesh, she grimaced.

"How could I let it get so out of hand?" she thought. Sissy turned so that her left side could be seen. Shaking her head at her profile and the overhanging flesh, she turned once more so her backside was in view. With her left hand, Sissy grabbed her butt cheek then released it. "This is so disgusting and ridiculous. It shouldn't have gotten to this point."

She walked over to her dresser and pulled out a pair of pajamas then quickly dressed. Climbing into bed, she pulled the sheet and thick comforter to her chest. When she reached over to turn off the bedside lamp, she noticed the new journal and ink pen that she'd purchased earlier at Barnes and Noble.

The thick leather book with its burgundy and gold embossed medieval design invited her to pick it up. She unbuckled the strap of the book, smiling as the spine cracked open. Sissy stared at the blank lined page, empty and ready to receive whatever secrets she wanted to confide. With pen in hand, she made her first entry:

What <u>was</u> I thinking when I suggested to my friends that we start a weight loss program? Is it the disgust I feel in myself that has triggered this, or do I really care about them? Angela and Nicki weren't too happy with me and I hope that this hasn't caused a rift in our relationship. Well, it's time to move on with or without them. To be fat or not to be fat, that is the question.

She closed the journal and thought, "Yeah, but what's the *answer*?" At the moment there wasn't one, so she laid the journal and pen on the bedside table and turned out the light. Patting her abdomen she said, "Goodnight buddy."

Angela removed the last vestiges of her MAC make-up while starring at her plain face in the mirror. "What the blank had gotten into Sissy?" she thought while trying to use alternate words to curb her cursing habit. "All of a sudden she wants to start some health kick for some strange reason."

"I wonder," she said to the mirror, "if she's met some guy and wants to look sexy for him?" As far as Angela was concerned, if a man couldn't accept you for yourself then *bump* him. Cody, her boyfriend of eight months, enjoyed Angela's size eighteen frame, fat rolls and all. He never complained nor asked her to lose weight. She twirled a large lock of hair into a bun then repeated the act on a second lock.

"She needs to keep that mess to herself," she said aloud.

"What did you say baby?" a male voice called out. Angela walked out of the bathroom in an ankle length emerald green silk gown. The delicate lace dipped into a deep V revealing her large breasts. She sat beside Robert on the edge of the bed,

"Oh, nothing. I mean, Sissy brought up some stupid thing about losing weight and stuff. I told her that you were proud of what you had."

He leaned in and kissed her. "Yeah, I love my big girl," he said as he grabbed the top of her thigh. His hand slid down to the end of the gown, grabbing a handful of the material, pushing it up towards her hips. Her legs parted slightly while he dropped to his knees, kissing her thighs back and forth. "Don't lose weight baby. I like you just the way you are," and he opened her legs wider with his hands. She let out a deep breath, "I won't," then laid back allowing him to take control.

Nicki pulled her legs up on the couch placing the bowl of popcorn in her lap. With the remote control in her right hand she punched in forty-seven, Turner Classic Movies. *Waterloo Bridge* with Robert Taylor and Vivian Lee had just begun. She popped several kernels in her mouth although she wasn't hungry.

"Am I eating out of boredom or loneliness?" The flicker of light from the television engulfed the dark room providing the comfort she needed. Nicki stared at the beautiful actress on the screen and dreamt it was her with the slim figure.

Why did Sissy have to open her big mouth about losing weight? It was the last thing Nicki wanted to think about. She had already come to the conclusion that her size twenty-two figure was the way it was meant to be, a string of failed diets proved that. Besides, she had long since learned how to ignore the rude comments people made when they thought she was out of earshot:

"She has such a pretty face, but oh that body!"

"What a shame, a beautiful face but such a big butt."

On the television screen, Taylor and Lee, were on the dance floor, gazing into each other's eyes while the band played in the background. Nicki smiled and wondered what it would be like to have a man who enjoyed looking at you, saying how beautiful you are. Although she didn't want to admit it, Sissy was right, they needed to lose weight.

"I'm thirty years old and haven't been on a date in five years! Who would want me like this?" Suddenly she lost her taste for the popcorn and placed the bowl on the coffee table. Nicki stretched out on the couch, propped a couple throw pillows under her head and continued to watch the movie. A moment later, something wet touched her lips. She closed her eyes and sobbed silently while the movie played on.

three

"This scale must be wrong!" Sissy shouted while glaring at the bright red digital numbers flashing at her. Stepping off the scale and allowing it to reset, she stepped on it again. She groaned and kicked the dusty metal enemy that flashed 185 pounds as her current weight.

She snatched her yoga pants and a large tank top from the back of the bathroom door and quickly dressed. Tying up her workout shoes, she still fumed at the "bad news" on the bathroom scale. Ear buds in place, the front door slammed as she left the house and started her power walk. Songs from Maroon 5, Nicki Minaj, and Rihanna blared in her ears. Her pace eventually slowed when her winded breathing proved that she was sorely out of shape. Sissy's anger gradually dissipated as she struggled around the walking course.

Thirty minutes later she stepped back in the house, cooled down with a couple of stretches, then retrieved her journal and sat down with a protein shake in hand. Opening the journal to a new page, she wrote:

June 8, 2012
I have to face the fact that I am out of shape and only hurting myself. The scale said 185, and that hurts. Went on my first walk and felt heavy and slow. When I saw my shadow on the ground, it looked like a blob; shapeless and ugly. I could only walk for thirty minutes before calling it quits. How sad at the age of 45! Seems like the only boyfriend I'll ever have is the abdominal fat around my middle that follows me wherever I go.

—∞—

Nicki pulled into the parking lot of the restaurant. She loved the Waffle House and it loved her back. She pushed through the glass doors as waitresses called out greetings and food orders.

"Welcome to Waffle House," a pudgy waitress with honey brown hair called out. She turned to face one of the food stations and said, "Kim, pull one chicken; mark, chicken and eggs over well." One cook stood near the waffle/toast station while two others handled different sections of the grill.

Orders continued to bounce back and forth like a tennis match from opposite ends of the cooking stations.

"Side of Texas toast, two sausages," said another waitress on the left side of the grill.

"Pull one bacon, mark, scramble egg and cheese. Drop one hash brown, smothered and covered," a slender waitress with a droopy top knot yelled out over the din of conversation.

Nicki made her way to an empty booth in the back of the restaurant. A waitress approached the table. Her black and white striped apron was a painter's canvas of egg splatters, cheese, smeared butter and who knew what else. The chambray shirt and black pants were spotless by comparison. A brunette ponytail sat high on top of her head while the "WH" initialed visor was pulled low on her forehead. She looked tired, as though she were trying to wake up, or possibly finishing the night shift.

"Good morning. Would you like something to drink? Coffee, maybe?" Nicki smiled at the young girl's attempt to stifle a yawn while taking her order.

"No thank you. I'll have a small orange juice while I wait for my friend." The waitress scribbled on her notepad as she walked away.

Nicki noticed a couple in the booth that faced her. They laughed and snuggled up to one another. He was a large guy, maybe in his thirties, wearing a striped polo shirt. His baseball cap was turned backwards. It looked ridiculous perched high on his head like a misplaced crown. His round pudgy face sported three days' worth of stubble, as he chewed away on a toothpick that moved back and forth in his mouth.

His girlfriend broke into an annoying cackle whenever he whispered in her ear. Her dirty blonde hair swung from one side to the other with every silly joke he made causing a pair of sunglasses to slip from the top of her head, which she quickly pushed back into place. A long tattoo along her collar bone peeped out from the scoop neck tee shirt that she wore. When they started to lip lock, Nicki looked away, annoyed by their antics. She pulled a small notepad from her purse and jotted a few notes. "Dish detergent, toilet paper, and avoid sitting in areas where there are public displays of affection". Around the last item she placed several stars.

"Hey chick, what's up?" Sissy slid into the seat in front of Nicki blocking the love-starved couple.

"Oh, nothing much." She put the notebook away and picked up the placemat that doubled as a menu and flipped it over.

"Well I'm famished," Sissy said and looked at the young waitress as she returned to the table. "I'll take a hot tea, a waffle, more brown than blonde, and a side of sausage."

Nicki stared at her friend, surprised at how little she had ordered and felt slightly embarrassed when she placed her order. "I'll have the All American; two eggs over hard, sausage, grits, waffle and wheat toast". Once the girl stepped away Sissy started, "So what happened that you had to see me this morning?"

Nicki, slightly embarrassed, released the menu she was holding onto like a life raft and answered. "How serious were you about us losing weight?"

"Very. Why?"

"I'm beginning to think you're right." She paused for a moment, staring out of the window. The sun attempted to break through the clouds that were blocking its path. "Yesterday, I lost it during one of my movies. Maybe I'm just being hormonal. One minute I'm staring at the television screen and the next, I'm balling my eyes out. I found myself wishing that I were beautiful and having some guy tell me so."

"But you *are* beautiful, Nicki."

"It doesn't mean the same when you say it or when I say it to myself. No offense Sissy, but there's a certain rush that a woman gets when an attractive man says, you're beautiful."

Her friend smiled while nodding her head. "Believe or not, I do understand." After the waitress delivered their food, Nicki continued.

"They say big is beautiful, but it's not true for everyone. Angela is fine with it because she has a man that loves her for it, but that's not the case for me and my size twenty-two butt." She stabbed at a piece of waffle, stuffed it in her mouth and began to chew.

"So, what do you plan to do about it?"

"Have you started your diet?" Nicki asked between bites of bacon and eggs.

"I'm not calling it a diet, just a modification. For example, before coming here I walked for thirty minutes on the track."

"Oh man, I don't know if I could last five minutes let alone thirty."

"You go at your own pace Nicki. Today I felt better than I did last Monday when I could only do fifteen minutes, but with each day it gets better. I'm also starting to notice the small things around me."

"Like what?"

"Oh the pine trees along my walking path, how soft the needles are when I touch them or looking at the different stages of a pine cone before it hits the ground. At times, I notice the color of the sky or the clouds and their different formations."

Nicki pushed her dishes to the side after completing her meal. "So when you said you were starving, did it have anything to do with your exercising?"

"Believe it or not, it did. I feel good after my workouts although during the first week I was so tired because my body wasn't used to exercising." Sissy could almost see the wheels turning in Nicki's head. She hoped her friend would consider the plan and make an attempt to do something about her weight. Nicki was a sweetheart and deserved to be happy.

With her voice barely a whisper, Nicki admitted her biggest fear. "Sissy, I'm embarrassed to go out alone. I mean, I'm so ..." and she pointed to her large frame.

"Well, I'm not exactly a size six." Sissy sat back and laughed, and Nicki smiled, despite herself. They gathered their purses, walked to the counter and paid their bills. Stepping outside, the warm spring air was a welcome relief from the chill they'd felt after sitting in the air-conditioned restaurant.

Sissy placed her arm around her friend, squeezing her with a sideways hug. "When you're ready to do this thing for yourself, call me and we'll find a way to work out together."

Nicki brushed at the tear that threatened to descend down her cheek. "Thanks Sissy. I'm almost there."

⸙⸙⸙

Angela felt like a cat after a long nap as she stretched and moaned. Her muscles protested against even this slight bit of activity. Cody made her feel like a goddess after the exquisite sex that continued until three in the morning.

Yes, her baby knew how to take it to the next level of experimentation pushing her to the brink of destruction and then yanking her back to reality. She glided her hands on top of her thighs and sighed deeply at the thought of Cody's lovemaking.

Her eyes flickered, and then opened as she turned towards her left to find that he wasn't there. She scanned the room, unable to find any sign of his being there. Her clothes were strewn about; bra on the back of a chair, panties on the floor, stockings on the dresser. How in the world did they land there?

Pulling herself upright in bed, she drew the sheet to her chest, wondering why Cody hadn't awakened her before leaving. Just as an attitude was about to break forth, she heard the slow, sing song of a whistle at the bedroom door which slowly opened.

"Hi baby," the husky voice began. "Did you sleep well?" His slow sexy smile always drove her crazy.

She nodded demurely and said, "As well as can be expected."

"I thought you could use this." He handed her a cup of hot coffee sweetened with a splash of hazelnut creamer. In his other hand he held a green and white striped bag from her favorite bakery. "I picked up an orange and cranberry muffin for you."

"That's my baby, always thinking about me." He leaned in and kissed her while rubbing her lower back.

"You keep that up and you won't make it to work on time," she whispered then pulled away. With his forefinger, he tapped the tip of her nose. "I know, that's why I'm standing up and backing away. Besides I have a nine o'clock appointment this morning. I'll call you later. Love you, bye."

He stepped on the lacy, soft pink panties that lay on the floor, bent down, and picked them up. "See, this is what got you into trouble last night." He stuffed them into his pant pocket while walking out the door.

Leaning against the head board she shouted, "Just wait until I wear the midnight blue ones." She took a sip of coffee and closed her eyes while plotting her next sexcapade.

four

It was Saturday and the Fourth of July. What a great combination. The day was in full swing with seventy degree weather as the sound of cherry bombs and Black Cats exploded throughout the neighborhood. Sissy stepped out on the stoop of her townhouse, wearing denim Bermuda shorts and a blue and white cotton lightweight top while holding a glass of lemonade in her left hand. She sat on the first step and took a long swallow of the rich nectar as it washed away her thirst.

Placing the bright orange tumbler beside her, she then leaned forward, arms on top of her thighs. A pill bug inched by. She reached down and with the lightest touch, stroked the creature. Feeling threatened, it curled into a tight ball. She remembered her brother, William, being fascinated by the roly polys as they use to call them. "You know they are land-based crustaceans, not insects," he began. "Pill bugs can drink from their anus and their mouths."

Sissy remembered going to a dictionary to look up the word "anus" for fear of looking stupid in front of William and shuddered after reading the definition. From then on she asked him not to tell her anything else about the little creatures. She leaned back on her elbows and listened to the "pop," "pow," "bang" of the fireworks that seemed closer than before. Sissy concluded that her neighbor, Mrs. Rodgers, had the grandchildren with her today and was grateful for the privacy gate that surrounded her townhouse. The last thing she wanted to deal with was the prying eyes of a five and eleven year old.

All Sissy wanted was to be alone with her thoughts and memories of past Fourth of Julys. She remembered the hand-held sparklers and fountains that glowed in the night sky. These were her favorites. Her dad was such a kid at heart, always making a big deal over what would be discharged first and why.

"You and William go in the backyard and fire off the Black Cats, snakes and parachutes. You don't want to wait until dark to do these, otherwise you won't see them."

Sissy chuckled at the memory of her fingers stuck into her ears to ward off the loud noise, squealing with joy. William would let a string of Black Cats go off in rapid fire succession. Her least favorite, the snakes, kept her at a distance. It was William who finally coaxed her into striking a match and placing it on the grey, round tablet. A high, red-orange flame flickered and like magic a curling, black abstract figure would appear.

After a day full of picnics with relatives, late afternoon naps, and the drone of baseball announcers on the television, evening arrived and it was finally time for the grand finale. Charles Bakersfield was just as much of a child as his youngsters. As soon as he felt it was dark enough, he would gather the family and bags of fireworks and head to the backyard. His wife would sit in the lounge chair as he orchestrated the "greatest display you will ever see." Sissy loved the spray of colors, the sizzle and bang as fountains shot up high in the sky. Yes, it was all mystical, magical and the "greatest display ever" each year.

"Madame, I do believe you have a call," the talking ringtone on her cell roused Sissy from her reverie. It was her brother William.

"How kind of you to call," Sissy said with a mock British accent.

"Jolly, ho my dear," he replied and they both laughed. Ever since his move to London two years ago on a government contract, Sissy and William seemed to grow closer because of the distance. They made a pact that at least on holidays and birthdays they would call one another.

After catching up on family news and polite conversation, William became serious. "Sissy, I have a huge favor to ask of you."

"I'll try, if I can William."

"I feel like such a baby for admitting this, but I really miss home. I know mom and dad won't fly out here but would you consider coming?"

"What?" She couldn't believe his request.

"Would you consider flying to London for a week or so? Because of my work contract, I'm not allowed a month of leave until next year. I miss all of you so much that…

"Sissy cut him off before he could say another word. "I'd love it," she squealed.

William was so relieved that he busted out in laughter. "I could help you with your ticket, maybe pay half of it?

"Oh William, that would be great! Hey while I'm there, maybe I could pop over to Paris?

"You could, but that would be on you. I can't travel there except on the weekends when I'm not working."

"Hey wait a minute," Sissy said once she calmed down from the excitement. "When are you expecting me to visit? I'm currently on a contract at a hospital that won't end until the nineteenth of October. Let's not forget that I'll have to save some money, check my passport…"

"I know silly," William said without malice. "I wasn't expecting you next week. Let's say, nine months from today. That'll give both of us enough time to make our arrangements and save money."

"Oh, I can't wait; it will be so good to see you again."

"You too, sis."

"Oh my goodness," she said while thinking aloud. "This may be just the thing I need to light a fire under their butts. Hey," she whispered forgetting that her brother was on the phone, "what if I tell them if they lose five or ten pounds or start exercising…Yes!" she shouted. "Wait until I tell my girls!" she shrilled adding, "They'll love it!"

"Your girls?" William asked cautiously. "Sissy what are you talking about?"

She proceeded to explain the weight loss plan and the Fat Girls Club. He roared with laughter then said, "A trip to Paris would be great motivation for you guys to lose weight."

Sissy knew her brother was being kind. William had never criticized her about her increasing waistline, and she loved him for it, but she knew that he was concerned about her weight. He had always been active, playing tennis and basketball in high school and college. When he joined the Air Force, he always appeared trim, fit and handsome in his uniform, due in part to his regimen of daily running as well as preparation for half marathon competitions. She was sure that he was secretly happy that she was taking this big step.

"Well Sissy," he said, "I've got to go. Thanks for cheering me up today. I really needed it. I'll email you after I check flight information and a few other things. Remember, stick to your weight loss plan and nine months from now I expect to see a slimmer you at Heathrow Airport. And if your friends happen to tag along, that'll just give me more women to love."

"Whatever, you bum," she laughed. They said goodbye and disconnected.

"London and Paris," Sissy squealed again as she stomped her feet on the walkway. "The battle of the bulge is in full swing now," she said while the clatter of firecrackers continued to fill the air.

───◦8∞◦───

Nicki drove through the open gates of Swope Park, Kansas City, Missouri's largest municipal park; veering right on the asphalt drive, she passed Starlight Theatre. Glancing in its direction, she remembered attending a few performances at the outdoor venue. That was before *it* happened.

She followed the twists and turns of the road until a pond appeared about a mile from the zoo's entrance. Nicki pulled the car into the first available space she could find. After all, it was a holiday and all 1,805 acres of the park buzzed with activity. Everywhere she looked there were picnics, music, children's laughter and the unnerving sound of exploding fireworks. The oppressive smell of gunpowder filled the air. After pushing a button on the car door, the windows glided down and Nicki clicked off the ignition.

She reclined the car seat slightly while watching the buzz of activity to her left at shelter house number twelve. It seemed like at least eight families were in the group, some were at the picnic tables that held several dark pots in various sizes. Two orange Igloo coolers blocked her view of the other items on the table. Lawn chairs, blankets and recliners dotted the hilly and misshapen sections of grass. It was nice to see so many people having fun.

Nicki reached across the console to the passenger seat and picked up the box of Kentucky Fried Chicken. She opened the flap and stared at the five-piece "original recipe" meal. After choosing a drumstick, she took a quick bite then reached for a paper bag that occupied the same seat. She returned the partially eaten chicken to the box, and from the bag, pulled out containers of mashed potatoes with gravy, coleslaw and string beans. Removing the lids, Nicki placed them on the dashboard then reached for another box. "KFC has the best biscuits around," she said to herself while preparing one of the golden brown delights with butter and strawberry jam. Without hesitation, she wolfed down the bread then finished off the drumstick. She washed it all away with big gulp of Fanta strawberry soda. While eating from one of the small containers, her mind drifted to the event that turned what was once a fun holiday for her into a bleak and regretful one. That was thirty or forty pounds ago when she was smaller and attractive. Her head fell against the headrest as she thought of the time when she dated Michael Malone.

Michael worked as a full time employee at the Ford Plant in Claycomo, Missouri. He served as a weekend warrior every month in the Army Reserves. Nicki remembered that there was a certain something about him that made her smile when she noticed him at the entrance of the local Sears store. "What was it?" she said aloud.

A 'thud' on the hood of her car startled her.

"Sorry lady!" a chorus of young voices piped. Four children scrambled for the bright orange and blue ball then ran up the hill. Nicki waved at the lone child that was still near her car as he scrambled off to try to catch up with the older children. He gave a quick wave then with a successful attempt at the incline, joined his friends.

Nicki looked at the empty food containers, embarrassed that she had devoured the contents without a conscious thought. In fact, three pieces of chicken and all the biscuits had disappeared. She dumped the Styrofoam bowls into the paper bag when she suddenly remembered what it was about Michael, his eyes. Those round soft brown eyes had mesmerized her, drawing her into the danger zone of his heart, capturing her with his lies — resulting in the one deep secret she had never told anyone.

⸺⸱⸱⸱⸱⸱⸺

Angela shook the bottle of soft baby pink fingernail polish as the gentle click-clack of the silver beads inside moved back and forth to mix the color. Her baby would soon pick her up for some Fourth of July summer fun. She placed the bottle on the table after unscrewing the cap. Poising the brush at the base of her cuticle, she gently glided it to the tip of her thumb nail. Once the entire nail had been painted, Angela paused momentarily to admire her work then moved on to the next finger.

"I'll be so happy when Cody gets paid so I can make my appointment at TOO HOT beauty salon," she said between soft blows of air across her nails to speed up the drying process. She had to admit that she had been spoiled by the monthly mani-pedis she received at the salon; Cody also paid for her bi-monthly hairdresser appointments.

"Humpf," she grunted while tossing the locks of hair over her right shoulder with her unpolished hand. "I can't believe he limited me to every two months for my hair. My weave needs to be washed and tightened on the regular." Angela was still complaining about the arrangements when the doorbell rang and the front door opened. A husky male voice called out.

"Hey Angela, where are you baby?"

"In the library, sweetie."

When Cody called an hour ago to let her know he was on his way, she'd unlocked the door so she wouldn't have to stop working on her nails. The polish had finally dried on her right hand when he stepped into the room. He placed a gentle kiss on her forehead and looked around at what was once the dining room.

"Hey, you did a great job in here," Cody said while reaching for a book that sat on a side table. "When you told me that you were going to remodel this area I didn't believe it would work. Now I have to admit that I'm really impressed."

The walls were painted in alternating colors of linen white and antique red, breaking the monotony of the room's prior single color scheme. The chaise lounge was upholstered in champagne pink chintz covered with bright roses. The philodendron that she had nursed for ten years spilled out of a Victorian plant stand to the right of the entrance. Two sets of cherry wood bookcases, floor to ceiling in height, pressed against the walls. A stunning oak library ladder leaned in front of a set of bookshelves. Each shelf, nearly full, held groupings of ten to twenty books. Unique bookends, plants, large seashells and wonderful frames holding pictures of friends and families were inserted between the book settings. The whole room appeared softer and more feminine.

He pointed at two items, one inside the other, near the bookcases. "Where did you find that old top hat and cane?" his voice was full of wonder.

Angela, shocked that he even noticed said, "Sissy is a sucker for antique malls and theater warehouses. One Saturday, Nicki and I tagged along with her to a place called Back Two Quest Antique Mall, that's where I found those things. The building is an old shoe warehouse with four large floors of goodies. We had a blast, you feel like you're in a giant treasure chest."

He walked across the room to a tufted back chair in champagne pink and took a seat. "Hey, this is much more comfortable than it looks." Cody glanced at the brushed silver polished floor lamp and turned it on. He placed his right leg atop of his left kneecap and looked down at the floor. "Wow Angela, you pulled the carpet too?"

"Yeah, the old thing wouldn't work with the new color scheme, so I had cherry wood flooring installed. I love the sheen of it, and it complements the bookcases as well as the rest of the furniture." She walked over to him and he uncrossed his legs so she could sit in his lap. "You didn't know I was so talented did you?"

"Oh, I knew you were talented in more ways than one!" Cody drew her near, planting kisses on her eyelids and nose. After a heated, sensual kiss, he gave her bottom lip a tug.

She moaned softly then placed both hands on his white polo shirt and pushed away. "We better go before we miss the show."

Angela stood up quickly, stepped away from him then turned back around. "So, how do I look?" She did a slow model strut as though she were on the catwalk while showing off her beige capri pants and short-sleeve beige shirt. Pausing and sticking out her left foot, she wiggled the pink toenails that peeped out from the jeweled strapped thongs.

"If the sun hits those rocks just right, they could blind a person," he joked. Angela frowned and started to walk away. Cody jumped up and caught her by the arm pulling her into him. "Baby you know you look good so stop screwing up your face." He smacked her backside and said, "Now let's go."

As they headed to the front door, Angela grabbed her purse from the hall bench. They were in the foyer when she turned to tell Cody about the new restaurant she wanted to try and noticed him texting frantically on his cell phone.

"Is everything OK?" she asked, looking at the pained expression on his face.

"What? Oh, yeah, I'm good." He quickly changed the subject while sliding his Galaxy cell phone into the back pocket of his jean shorts. "Do you have everything, keys and purse?"

Angela held the mentioned items up for him to see before they stepped out the door onto the small porch. He pulled the door tight until the lock clicked then they made their way to the driveway.

"Wow, check you out," Angela's voice a tad louder than she planned. "When did you get this baby?" she asked as they walked closer to the car.

"I picked it up yesterday." He rubbed his hands over the Honda Accord sedan. The crystal black pearl color gleamed in the sun. Walking over to the passenger side of the car he opened the door for her. Angela ran her hand against the black fabric while glancing at the interior. It wasn't until they were settled in the car that Cody freely discussed his new purchase.

"This thing is a beauty and has so many features. Check this out. Wheel mounted controls, satellite navigation with voice recognition and rearview camera."

"Yeah, it's sweet," her voice betrayed her feelings. She was little miffed at the fact that he hadn't mentioned in their past conversations that he was considering a new car, let alone buying one. Just as quickly, she reprimanded herself for thinking such things. After all, his work as an Army JAG officer afforded him such luxuries; besides, they weren't married – yet.

He turned the ignition and slowly backed down the driveway. Once they were on their way, he surprised Angela with a change of plans. "I've decided that we'll go to Worlds of Fun."

"Cody, no, not the amusement park!" she protested. "What about my hair, my clothes? Some of those rides involve water."

"You're wearing a bra and panties aren't you?"

"Yeah, but…"

"As long as you're not sagging or dragging when your clothes get wet, we're golden. And as far as your hair goes, it's just a splash of water not the whole ocean," he laughed while merging the car into the highway traffic. Angela didn't find his joke so funny. She turned her head to the right and stared out the passenger window with a frown on her face. "OK, this dude is starting to tick me off," she fumed to herself, "first the new car, now this sudden change of plans – all without consulting me. And what was up with that text message? Is he up to something, or am I just making a big deal out of nothing?" She pushed down a rising feeling of doubt while resigning herself to make the most of the day.

Sissy was still reeling from yesterday's conversation with her brother when she called Nicki then Angela on her three-way line. She asked that they meet her at Panera's for lunch at one o'clock on Saturday for an exciting proposition.

"Proposition?" Angela repeated. "I'm a good girl. I don't turn tricks, especially in the winter."

"OK smart butt," Sissy said in an exasperated tone. "I have some exciting news."

"Don't pay any attention to Angela," Nicki interrupted. "She's still gassy from all that barbeque she ate yesterday."

"Anyway," Sissy laughed, "just meet me this Saturday, both of you." She quickly disconnected the call before either one of them could ask any questions.

five

Saturday morning arrived with gentle winds and a cool sixty-five degrees. By noon, the sun's invigorating rays had driven the temperature to eighty-eight. Sissy pulled into the first available parking space she could find in the almost full lot. She thought that the lunch crowd would have begun to thin out by now. She was grateful for the chocolate brown Honda Element that she named Molly. The car was not only reliable, but could also squeeze into tight spaces. In addition, the vehicle allowed her to cram it full with all the items she took with her on her travel assignments.

She stepped out of the car then reached behind the driver's seat for her straw tote bag. Sissy gathered the travel magazines and brochures that were on the backseat, stuffing them into the tote. She strolled up to the restaurant and stepped through the double glass doors and looked around for her friends amid the buzz of activity. The booths were occupied with people deep in conversations between bites of food. Study groups with laptops and tablets were scattered here and there. A baby wailed in the background while a couple of small children ran around their seating areas to the chagrin of their parents.

After a few minutes Sissy spotted her friends in the main dining area of the restaurant toward the back. She waved her hand to get their attention. As she approached the table Sissy noticed the clear plastic tumblers in each woman's hand while they slurped away at their drinks.

"Hey chicas, what's up?"

"Hunger pains," Nicki answered as she tapped the black buzzer disc in front of her that had one red light flashing inside.

"Sorry, but we just couldn't wait," Angela said apologetically.

"No worries, I'm good." Sissy slid the straw tote from her shoulders and placed it in the chair beside her. "I'll be back," and she turned and walked to the counter to place her order.

"Hi, welcome to Panera. May I take your order?" The waif-like cashier with a soft voice looked as though she were seventeen. Her oval shaped face and pale skin were devoid of the typical teenage acne. Instead, her complexion was smooth accentuating her soft grey eyes and black eyebrows.

"Hello. I think I'll take a half order of the Fuji apple chicken salad and a raspberry tea."

"And your side choice is a roll, chips or an apple."

"Chips."

"Will that be all, miss?"

"Yes, thank you." Sissy watched as the young lady whose name tag read, Alice, totaled up her purchase.

"That will be seven dollars even. Oh, do you have a Panera card?" Sissy handed the money and card to Alice and watched her complete the transaction. She took the receipt and change then stepped to the far end of the counter to wait for her food order.

After a few minutes, the disc in her hand buzzed as the red lights raced around the center. She dropped it in the nearby basket and picked up her tray, carrying it back to the table to join her friends. Once she settled into her seat she explained her surprise. Sissy recounted the phone call from William then finished the conversation with her suggestion of the trip.

"You're kidding?" Nicki said with her spoon perched midair over her potato soup.

"No ma'am. He wants me to fly over for a visit and I thought, why not all three of us."

"Girl, I can't just take off at the drop of a hat," Angela said after swallowing a bite of her sandwich.

"Look, Ms. Drama Queen," Sissy began, "I realize that. So we decided the trip would take place nine months from now. It would give us all time to submit our vacation requests before the available time slots are taken, as well as save our money."

"Nine months," Angela huffed, "that's the same amount of time is takes to have a baby."

"So are you trying to tell us something Angela," Nicki questioned her friend with raised eyebrows?

"Girl please, you better go somewhere with that mess. Angela doesn't do baby shoes or baby poop." The girls broke out in loud laughter then toned it down when several heads turned in their direction.

"OK, seriously," Sissy continued while gaining control of the conversation. "Check these out." She reached into her tote bag and pulled out several travel brochures and pamphlets, passing them out to the girls. Nicki "oohed" and sighed at the pictures while Angela pointed at the various tour packages and their prices.

"If I were to judge just by your reactions," Sissy began, "I'd say this trip is up for consideration."

"Possibly," Angela said cautiously. "I can understand why you want to go. You have a brother to look forward to but why should Nicki and I?"

"Well that's the part I haven't explained. I feel that this would be the perfect weight loss challenge. If we set our goal to lose a certain amount of weight and tone up, this would provide the perfect reason to do so. Think of it as the gold cup at the end of the race."

Nicki's eyes widened. "You mean we could celebrate our weight loss with you in Europe?"

"Of course," Sissy smiled.

Angela blurted out, "You want me to leave my honey to hang out with you guys for how long?"

"It's just a week or two. For goodness sake, it isn't the end of the world."

Angela continued to protest. "But still…"

"But nothing," Nicki interrupted. "Look, how many times have you flown to Europe?"

"None," Angela responded in a terse voice.

"Well then," Nicki looked at Sissy, "count me in. I would love to walk down the Champs Elysées or have a cup of coffee at an sidewalk café. Oh, and let's not forget the Louvre, and Sacré Coeur, and…"

"Hold up Nicki." Angela's hand flew into the air. "Do you honestly believe that you could lose what, thirty, twenty, even ten pounds in nine months?"

"Angela," Sissy hissed. "How dare you speak to her that way?" Nicki's eyes twinkled with tears that dared to surface.

"Look, I'm just being realistic just as she should be. And you're not helping by giving her these wild ideas."

"Why you…"

"No Sissy, I've got this." Nicki reached for a napkin on the table and dabbed at the tears that pooled at the rim of her eyes. She turned in her seat and leaned in close to Angela, lowering her voice so that what she had to say would not be overheard. "Look chick. Just because you've got someone loving up on your fat rolls, don't fool yourself into believing that Cody couldn't do better."

Angela's mouth hung open and Sissy gasped. This was a side of Nicki that neither woman had ever seen.

"So Ms. Thing, you walk around here swinging that fake hair around and flashing those fake nails because you believe they're yours. You're even stupid enough to believe that all he wants is your fat butt and that you don't have to do anything else to keep your man. Well Missy, your size eighteen plus, roly-poly behind will have a rude awakening one day. Angela, you better get ready for a bumpy ride. One morning you'll wake up in a cold, empty bed all by your lonesome. When that day comes, remember to ask yourself, 'Why did he get so tired of me?'"

Nicki turned her tear-stained face in Sissy's direction. "I'll go with you to Paris. I don't care if it's only ten pounds that I lose, at least I'll be ten pounds lighter than what I started with."

Before Sissy could respond, Nicki grabbed her purse, and plopped the travel booklets inside. She stood, excused herself from the table and with her head held high, headed out the front door and never looked back.

six

Angela stared in Sissy's direction. "I can't believe that heifer spoke to me like that. How dare she try to predict my future like a fortune teller."

"You better be glad that she didn't go street on you and cuss your behind out. What's wrong with you Angela? Nicki's been your friend for years. How could you have been so callous?"

"Sissy, you know that Nicki has tried too many times to lose weight and failed miserably. Why should you get her hopes up when you and I both know that it won't happen this time either?"

"Angela, shut up." Sissy gathered the remainder of the pamphlets and booklets, stuffing them into her tote. She was grateful that the restaurant crowd had dwindled, saving them from the embarrassment of witnesses to the fallout. She looked at Angela while placing the straw tote onto her left shoulder.

"You need to apologize to Nicki and in the future, learn to keep your negative and defeatist comments to yourself."

She picked up her tray and Nicki's, and walked to the trash container. One of the staff members stopped her and took them from her hands. Before walking out, she glanced back at Angela, shook her head and pushed the glass door open and walked out.

"Oh well," Angela muttered to herself. "Some people just can't handle the truth." She took another bite from her sandwich while turning a page in the travel magazine.

On the fourth ring, Nicki finally answered her cell phone.

"Hey girl, it's Sissy. Where are you? You ran out of the restaurant and were gone before I could catch up with you."

"Why?"

"Don't do this Nicki. Where are you?" Sissy insisted.

"I'm a block away at Sonic."

"I'll be there." Sissy hung up before Nicki could protest and drove the short distance to the drive-in. She parked her car and walked over to her friend's then knocked on the passenger window. When she heard the locks click she opened the door and settled into the car seat.

Sissy turned slightly to face Nicki then her eyes moved to the banana split container that sat in her friend's lap. "Baby girl, what are you doing?" Sissy cautiously asked.

"What do you think?" Nicki snapped. "I'm a big girl so I'm feeding my big gut."

"So you're going to prove to that knucklehead Angela that she was right?"

Nicki stuffed another spoonful of ice cream into her mouth to avoid answering Sissy's question. The two sat quietly in the car as the music from the outside speakers played the tune, "Quicksand", by Martha Reeves and the Vandellas.

The voice of a man in a faded black Toyota truck parked in the next stall could be overheard. He shouted his order of a "Number One" with tater tots and large cherry limeade through the speaker as though the people on the other end were deaf. Nicki finished off the last bit of ice cream and put the container in the white paper bag that had fallen to the floor of the car. She sat up, averting her eyes from Sissy choosing to keep them transfixed on the windshield.

"So, was that banana split worth it?" her friend asked.

"I just didn't care anymore. Who am I fooling, Sissy? You and I know that I've taken the weight loss road before without success."

"That was then, girl. Now you have something to shoot for. It's not only a chance to feel better but think of all the fun we'll have. We'll visit the Louvre and the Eiffel Tower. Imagine sipping coffee at the sidewalk cafés and shopping in French boutiques."

When her friend didn't answer, Sissy looked to her left and noticed the tears streaming down Nicki's face.

"Sissy," she said in a small voice. "I didn't even want that stupid ice cream. I ate it out of spite and anger. It was a punishment."

"But a punishment for whom, Nicki? It didn't hurt me and it definitely didn't put a dent in Angela's game."

Nicki giggled between the tears that coursed down her cheeks while she blew her nose. "Yeah, I guess I showed her."

Sissy reached over and held Nicki's hand. In a low conspiratorial voice she said, "Now if you really want to get back at Ms. Beauty Queen, do the opposite. Start eating right and exercising. I promise, when that weight begins to fall off, watch out; Angela will have a fit. You must understand that it will *not* be easy, nothing worth having ever is, but you'll feel so much better."

Nicki nodded her head and Sissy noticed the beginning of a smile. "Oh, one more thing," she added. "If you need me, call me. Remember, I'm here for you."

"I love you Sissy. What would I do without you?"

"I love you too. Now, let's get out of this place." Sissy opened the car door, stepped out and just before she shut it, gave her friend a thumbs-up. As Sissy walked back to her car she let out a deep sigh then reached up to wipe away a tear that clung to her chin.

Nicki crossed the threshold and pressed the toggle switch to turn on the lights. She walked into her living room, placing her purse and jacket in the nearby Bentley styled chair. Still keyed up from the events of the past few hours, first Angela then Sissy, she stepped into the bedroom and changed into her burgundy lounging outfit.

She returned to the living room while tightening the sash on her bath robe. Reaching into the pocket she removed a small notebook and black ink pen then sat down on the couch in front of her.

Sissy said that writing down her feelings helped her stay focused and that she should try it. "I'm no writer," she told Sissy.

"It's not a novel that you're creating," she laughed. "Just use it to put your thoughts in place."

Nicki perched the pen on the first line and began to jot a few words.

I can't tell anyone my secret. No, not even my girls. The fear of losing their friendship is too strong. It's stronger than the secret itself.

That's all she could write and closed the notebook placing it and the ink pen on the coffee table. Nicki drew her legs up placing her feet on the sofa. She reached for the remote and pressed the "on" button. She wanted to close out the rest of the world and not think of weight, diets or the trip. All she wanted was Robert Osborn and Turner Classic Movies to drown out her loneliness. Ah, one of her all-time favorites, *Now Voyager* was playing.

Nicki could relate to the story of the ugly duckling that turned into a swan and found her way in the world. Like the main character Charlotte Vale, she too felt unattractive and couldn't remember the last time a man had asked her for a date. Even the word 'date' sounded like a foreign concept to her. Ever since the mishap with Michael, she'd buried her pain with food, growing bigger and more unappealing with each bite. Nicki could count on both hands and toes how many diets she'd tried in the past and failed.

She would lose five maybe ten pounds, then the dreaded "plateau" would occur followed by frustration until, finally, she would end the diet and return to her old eating habits. Even if, or when, people noticed her, they dissected her like a lab specimen. "Oh she has a beautiful face..." or "Her eyes are so big and alluring..." or the best one yet, "She wears her hair in the cutest styles that really flatter her."

Nicki was never whole; there was never a comment about her body, at least in a positive way. She knew the answer to her own question. Her obesity made her a misshapen beast in other people's eyes. She ate her pain and now it was killing her.

It wasn't until Sissy called the trio, "The Fat Girls Club", that she realized the impact of the words. Her attention returned to the movie. It was now at the scene when Bette Davis, or rather Charlotte Vale, made her way down the gang plank of the cruise ship onto the tender (a small boat), emerging from her cabin after days of not having been seen by the other passengers on board.

The camera focused at first on her spectator pumps, white with black tips. Seductively it glided up the front of her stockings until the shot widened to reveal her slender, shapely figure. At the last minute there was a pause as Charlotte's lovely face filled the frame. The butterfly had emerged from the cocoon of her former fat self.

"That will be me one day," Nicki said aloud. Silently she made a vow to Sissy that she would walk twenty to thirty minutes a day at least four times a week. Like Charlotte Vale, Nicki was going to be beautiful, loved and most of all happy with herself once again.

<hr>

Sissy stood near the stove and couldn't believe she'd survived Saturday and lived to see Sunday morning. She turned on the gas, watched the flames leap upward, and placed the silver tea kettle on the burner then rummaged in the cabinet to the left for her favorite tea cup and saucer.

The past twenty-four hours had resulted in tears, anger and insults. It was an emotional playground that she didn't care to play on again. Sunday is supposed to be a day of rest, and she planned to take full advantage of it. Walking to the front door, she opened it and then glanced to the left and right. She didn't want anyone to see her in the comic print pajamas.

She quickly pushed the screen open and grabbed the thick Sunday paper.

After making a cup of cranberry tea, Sissy sat at the dinette with a poppy seed muffin. She pulled out the entertainment section from the newspaper. On page three she noticed an ad for the Kansas City Improv located in the Zona Rosa shopping district. The "Queen of Comedy", K.K. Karen, was in town for a two day engagement with Sunday as the last day. After all that had happened yesterday, Sissy was convinced that she needed laughter; the deep, unrestricted kind of laughter that left you shaking your head. Before she had a chance to talk herself out of it, she jumped up, grabbed the cordless phone, punched in the number to the comedy club, and booked her reservation for the seven p.m. show.

seven

S issy's hands ran over her generous hips as she looked back at her reflection. "Not bad," she thought then turned to the side. The five pounds that she lost didn't really show in the mirror, but there was no denying the reduction that registered on the bathroom scale. She hurried to the bedside table and picked up the journal that sat on top and quickly jotted down a note.

While standing in my panties and bra, I can't see a difference in my weight or shape. The bathroom scale says that I'm five pounds lighter, but I don't feel it. I continue to walk but soon I'll have to join a gym for the variety of machines that they offer. As the seasons change I'll need a place to continue my workouts. The use of treadmills, bikes, rowing machines and exercise classes will keep the monotony at bay. No matter what, I'll try to stay positive and stick to my program. It's not only for my well-being, but I need to set an example for Nicki. Since I started this whole weight loss thing I have to prove to her that what I say is true. A healthy body leads to a healthy life. One of my favorite actresses, Mae West says, "It's better to be looked over than overlooked." That's my goal, to be smaller, healthier and sexier.

Sissy closed the journal and replaced it on the nightstand. She returned to the closet and pulled on a pair of flair leg, dark blue slacks and a sleeveless shirt, then searched the shelves above the clothes rack and removed a cobalt blue shawl to take with her. From her hanging shoe rack, she pulled out a pair of navy pumps, placed them on the floor and stepped into them. Racing around the corner to the bathroom, she clipped a pair of silver earring studs to her lobes, placed a small, sterling silver watch on her left wrist and peered at the dial, "Six o'clock, time to go!"

Sissy drove around the corner and located the parking garage. She pulled into a stall while noticing that there were not as many cars in the area and wondered if she'd made a mistake in the location of the comedy club. "Oh well, I'll just have to hoof it," she said aloud while closing the car door.

As she hurried across the street, the blare of a car horn frightened her. The driver swerved just in time to miss hitting her. She stepped onto the sidewalk and quickened her pace in search of the club, when suddenly her right foot wedged into a raised crack in the pavement, sending Sissy flying through the air like a super hero. The only thing she was missing was a cape! She landed on the hard surface with a thud and a wave of embarrassment. "Blank, blank, blank!" she repeated, trying not to swear. Before she had a chance to get to her feet, a pair of thick hands encircled her waist.

"Are you hurt," a deep, muted voice asked while assisting Sissy to her feet. She scrambled backward until her backside bumped into his stomach. Feeling even more embarrassed by this new blunder, she jerked her body upright.

He stepped into her view and Sissy unconsciously let out a low gasp. His face was the color of a caramel latte. There appeared to be a smidgen of light freckles along his cheeks and the bridge of his nose. His square jaw was firm as he awaited her answer while still holding her at the waist. She cleared her throat and stepped backward to release herself from his grasp.

His mouth was agape when he dropped his hands and said, "I'm sorry. I saw you take that fall and thought I'd help."

"Oh, um, I'm grateful," she stuttered while staring at his mouth. It was a delicious one indeed; thick lips ripe and ready for kissing…

what in the world was she thinking? Just as she was about to speak, he stepped to her left to pick up the clutch that still lay on the sidewalk.

"A few things fell out but I think I got them all. You may want to check," he said while handing it to her.

"Wow, what a mess." Sissy immediately brushed away the dirt on her clothes. "I'm so embarrassed. I know I look like some escaped convict."

"Not really," he smiled.

"Well, I've taken up enough of your time." When she looked up, his deep-set eyes stared back at her. They were luminous and velvet brown in color. Sissy felt drawn to him and yet it was all so crazy and unreal.

"Are you sure you'll be alright?"

"Of course, and again, thank you." She stuck her hand out to shake his but swiftly drew it back when she noticed the grime on her palm.

He chuckled. "Well, take care," he said then stepped out of her path and walked away. Sissy watched as his erect, confident stride proceeded up and around the corner to the left.

"What a hottie, and now he's gone!" She stomped her right foot and then grimaced. "Great! I've probably messed up my ankle and knee," Sissy grumbled as she gingerly ambled to the corner, looked right then left, and finally noticed the sign that announced the Improv.

Once Sissy stepped inside the lobby and down a narrow hallway, she tried to follow the host as he buzzed around tables to find a seat for her.

"Would you mind slowing down," she called after him. "I fell earlier on the sidewalk a few minutes ago and my knee and hip are really bothering me."

"Oh, sorry about that." He slowed his pace then guided her to a table near the stage. He watched as she carefully lowered herself into the chair.

"Now you won't have to walk so far to the lobby or restrooms which are right outside the door," he said before turning to leave. She thanked him and proceeded to straighten herself in the seat when she realized that there were two women seated at her table and giving her 'the eye.' It was if they wanted to say, "Why don't you take your butt somewhere else"

Their manner of dress hinted that they had been waiting on the man of their dreams to sit in the very chair that she had taken. The woman on the left had too much breast protruding from her black, low cut V-neck dress. It appeared that Victoria's Secret was working overtime to hold those puppies up. Her buddy sitting at her right seemed to have a water-fall coming out of the red, scooped neck dress she wore while her honey blonde weave cascaded over her chest like a Slip N' Slide water ride.

Sissy said, "Hello" and the two women curtly returned the greeting then continued their conversation. She fixed her attention to the stage as a projector flashed on the wall the next round of upcoming performers for the month. A mix of smooth jazz and contemporary music drifted around the room as people continued to fill the club. Conversations and laughter resonated throughout the small dining area and for a brief moment, Sissy wished that the man that had helped her to her feet were with her.

"What a foolish thought," she said to herself and reached into her purse and pulled out a notebook and a pen. She began to jot notes of what clothes to pack and the places she wanted to visit in London and Paris.

The girls always teased her about packing so early when a trip was still three or more months away. They would have had a field day if they could see her making a list right now, a full nine months in advance of their trip! Fifteen minutes later, a voice over an intercom welcomed everyone to the Improv and introduced their guest, K.K. Karen.

———— ◈◈◈ ————

The comedienne strutted on stage in a soft peach, lightweight top and matching pant. The beige stilettos that she wore made Sissy cringe. She rubbed her knee after imagining herself standing in those heels.

The show lasted an hour and a half and was well worth the ticket price. Her skits included a rant about Beyoncé's big hair and women driving and parking trucks like a man (unfeminine). She touched on other subject matter regarding dating, news headlines and even her own life. There was laughter, head shaking and high-fives throughout the area. Sissy guffawed at times to the point of tears. It was this type of deep from the belly laughter that she needed to erase the cares of the job from her mind. Even the 'snub sisters' interacted with Sissy once or twice during the evening. When the house lights went up and the music resumed, the guests lined up for a chance to have photos and autographs with K.K. Karen. Some people even purchased her comedy CD that was for sale at an adjoining table.

Sissy chose to wait until the line had dwindled down a considerable amount before making an attempt to approach the stage for an autograph. Just as she rose and took a few steps forward, she saw *him.*

He walked in front of Sissy and paused. "Well, well. So we have something in common." She smiled and nodded then the two stepped aside to allow a couple to pass.

"I wanted to get an autograph from K.K. Karen before she leaves," Sissy said as she tried to take another step.

"Why don't you sit here," he pulled out a chair and helped her in it, "and let me do that for you," he insisted.

Sissy watched as he made his way back to the stage holding the small notebook she had given him. He was talking to the comedienne for a bit when she noticed K.K. Karen leaning forward and began to wave in her direction. "I hope you start to feel better. Thanks for coming to my show," she yelled out.

Sissy waved in return. "I loved it."

He returned and showed Sissy the message that was written. "In show business the saying is break a leg, not break your butt!" They both laughed then noticed the activity around them as wait staff bused the remaining tables. The guests were almost non-existent and the music stopped suddenly.

"I better help you to your car to make sure you'll be safe."

"That would be nice but could I ask one question of you?"

"Sure, what?"

"It would be nice to know the name of the stranger that's been so good to me!"

He grinned then apologized. "I'm sorry. My name is Robert, Robert Douglas. My friends call me Red."

"Hello Red and my friends call me Sissy." They exchanged handshakes just as the manager called out, "OK ladies and gentlemen. We must close for the night. Thanks for coming to the Improv and we look forward to seeing you again."

"Oops," Red said. "We better go before they put us out on the sidewalk."

"I think I've already been there," Sissy joked. They laughed as she stood and with the aid of his left arm, limped down the short hall that led to the lobby and then out the front door.

Once he made sure she was settled into the car and had started the ignition, he looked at her for a moment before asking the question he'd been pondering during their walk. "So Sissy, are you dating anyone?"

"No I'm not. It's been awhile. What about yourself?"

"It's been a year for me." There was silence as the two glanced away.

"Well," he began, "I wanted to know if I could call you sometime. You know, to check on your knee."

She looked in his direction. "To check on my knee? Well, I'm disappointed that you only want to check out one of my body parts. I mean, oh man, that didn't come out right!"

"That's OK," he said and smiled broadly at the thought of what she had just said. He cleared his throat, "I know what you meant. But to set your mind at ease I really want to check *you* out."

Sissy couldn't speak for a moment but once she found her voice she said, "And the feeling is mutual." He leaned in through the window and kissed her cheek. She scribbled down her phone number on a sheet of paper from her memo pad and handed it to him. Red recited his number to her and watched while she jotted it down then checked that it was correct.

He backed away from the car. "I'll call you in a few minutes to make sure you made it home safely." He waved while holding the paper with her number on it.

She returned the gesture then pushed the button to roll up the window and drove off. Red was the last thing she saw in her rearview mirror when she exited the parking garage.

eight

Angela snatched her cell phone from the bedside table and pressed the unlock button to quiet the chime.

"Whoever's calling at this time of the morning better be my mama, my poppa or a very close friend, otherwise, you *will* be cussed out," she yelled into the phone before placing it to her ear.

"Why do you have to be so evil?" Sissy asked.

"Because it's eight in the morning and I haven't seen Cody in a week. Oh, and by the way, good morning."

"Good morning O Evil One."

"Whatever," Angela snorted. "So what's up?"

"I need to speak to you and Nicki this evening."

"Whoa sister girl, what's your hurry? I need some details."

"Nope. I don't want to spill anything until later. So don't ask because I won't tell."

"OK, secret keeper." Angela laughed.

Sissy continued. "Let's have dinner at Freddy's this evening."

"That's cool. Which one and what time?"

"How about the Freddy's off of 118th St. and Black Bob Rd. at seven."

"That's fine," Angela said while reaching for a short sleeved, navy coat dress for work. "It'll give me time to finish up with my second client."

"Good. Before I forget," Sissy decided to go for broke, "did you apologize to Nicki?"

Angela hesitated then confessed the truth. "I tried Sissy, but she's still upset with me."

"You think?" Sissy blurted out. "After what you said to her I'm surprised she took your call."

"I know, I know. Look, I'll try again at the restaurant this evening."

"I don't want any mess out of you Angela," Sissy's tone was firm and unwavering.

"You won't. Look, I need to finish dressing for work. I'll check you later."

"Later."

Sissy knew her next call would be difficult but proceeded anyway. On the third ring Nicki answered. "Hey Sissy, what's wrong."

"Nothing's wrong. Why do you ask?"

"It's eight-thirty in the morning, I'm walking into the front door of my job and you're calling me."

"I wanted to invite you to dinner this evening to talk about a couple of things," she paused for a moment then pressed on, "Angela will be there."

"What? Oh, hell no!" Nicki said just a bit too loud as one of her co-workers turned her head in Nicki's direction.

"Nicki, please, for me? Besides, Angela wants to apologize."

"I'd rather clean up dog dodo in the park than deal with Angela."

"Nicki that's a bit extreme."

"Well, that's how I feel," she said firmly.

Sissy found the stress between her friends grinding on her nerves. "Look, I need this love/hate thing to end between the two of you. I have something I want to share with both of you."

"What is it?"

"Nope, I'm not telling until tonight. So meet me at Freddy's on 118th and Black Bob Rd. around seven. If you love me you'll do it."

"OK, you brat," Nicki said.

"That's my girl. I'll see you later and have a good day."

"Bye," Nicki said before ending the call and slipping her cell phone in her jacket pocket. She reached over to her desktop computer, turned it on and watched it come to life. "That girl better be glad I love her," she said under her breath and began reading the memo that popped up on the screen.

With the approach of evening, the clouds took on a bluish grey color. Small rain droplets threatened to change into a downpour.

It was Wednesday evening, that half and half point of the week. Two days from the start of the work week and two days away from the weekend. Sissy walked through the glass doors of Freddy's and expected to find full tables and a line for dinner. Instead, it was the opposite. Probably ten people were in the whole restaurant. "What Doesn't Kill You" by Kelly Clarkson blared overhead.

A chipper, medium built blonde, that looked no more than sixteen, stepped behind the register. "May I help you?"

"I'm waiting on some friends." The girl nodded and walked away.

Sissy slid into one of the upholstered red cushioned booths. A white and red tile mix extended from the top of the seating while a bright red, metal industrial style lamp hung low reflecting a soft beam of light onto the black table top. She was staring at the big blocks of grey and off-white floor squares when Angela's size eight black pumps stepped into her view. "What are you trying to do, hypnotize yourself?" she asked.

"And it's good to see you too," Sissy said in a mocking tone.

"Of course it is," Angela responded as she snapped her fingers. When her friend righted herself, Angela kissed her cheek.

"Just remember what I told you Angela, behave and apologize."

"OK little mama." Just then Nicki stepped through the door, looked around and walked over to the booth to join her friends.

"Hello Angela," she said in a flat tone then sat next to Sissy.

"Hi Nicki. Look, before we get started, I want to say that I'm really sorry about my behavior the last time we were together. I was trying to make a point but it came across all wrong."

"It sure did."

"I know and I want to squash this anger between us. I love you Nicki and I only want the best for you."

"You're forgiven this time, but next time I'll try to beat you down if you ever speak to me like that again." Nicki raised her left fist for emphasis.

"Yikes!" Sissy blurted out.

Angela smiled and then said, "You've got a deal." The two shook hands.

"Now that we have that under wraps, let's order our food," Sissy insisted as she playfully pushed Nicki out of the booth. The three walked to the counter. Nicki ordered a grilled chicken breast sandwich, while Sissy and Angela went for the single steak burger California style combos. Nicki volunteered to eat some of Sissy's french fries. They took turns at the soda fountain, gathered soufflé cups of catsup then returned to their booth until their number, two eighty-seven, was called.

Robert sat at the desk in his trailer at the construction site. It served as his makeshift office and library. It was Wednesday evening. The machines sat motionless and the work crew had dispersed. He couldn't quite get the last column of the payroll sheet to balance and it was starting to wear on him. Once again he punched the numbers into the adding machine. It wasn't until he totaled the last column of figures that he realized his mistake.

"Finally," he said with an exhaustive sigh when the tally and the payroll sheets balanced. He threw the ink pen on the desk, leaned back into the swivel chair and closed his eyes. "What's wrong with me?" It had been months since Robert had felt so out of his game as during the past seventy-two hours. He felt frazzled, unable to concentrate on the business at hand. Even a few of the guys on the construction team told him that he looked tired and complained about the smallest things.

If he were honest with himself he could answer his own question. It was Sissy, the woman he helped Sunday. A smile covered his face when he thought of her fine tush as it backed into his stomach when he tried to help her up. Yes, she definitely piqued his interest. When she turned around, he noticed her heart shaped face. And how could he forget those smoldering black eyes that made him want to hold onto her a little longer.

Suddenly, Robert's eyes flew open and he sat upright. "What am I doing? This is *not* the time to think about a woman in terms of dating or otherwise," he tried to convince himself aloud. "I have a business to run, contracts to honor and completion dates to beat."

For ten years, The Robert Douglas Construction Company had held a good reputation in and around the Kansas City Metro area as well as some of the surrounding counties. This was due to his workaholic nature and fair trade practices — and not to some woman whose conversation he had enjoyed on a late Sunday evening.

It had been awhile since he'd relished talking and laughing with an intelligent female. In fact, the brief phone call to check that Sissy had made it home safely lasted an hour and half with both of them reluctantly hanging up because each had to work the next day.

Robert swore briefly while snatching up the paperwork on the desk. Why did Sissy have to show up now? Hadn't his ex-fiancé taught him anything? After their split, the year he spent by himself gave him the opportunity to learn how *not* to depend on someone else to be the source of his happiness, while his work kept him sane. "Been there, done that," he said as he quickly stuffed the files into his leather messenger bag, jabbed his arms through the sleeves of the coat hanging on the back of the office chair, and grabbed the black newsboy cap from his desk. "Got to get out of this stuffy place and clear my head." He paused long enough at the front door to check that his keys were in his coat pocket, "Women! What a distraction!" he shouted as the door slammed behind him.

The girls were halfway through their meals when Nicki said, "So Sissy, what was so important that you wanted to meet with us this evening?"

"Well," she began, "besides missing your company, I wanted to make sure that you and Angela got your act together."

"We've had a meeting of the minds," Nicki volunteered and raised her left eyebrow.

"Yeah, yeah, were cool," Angela confirmed.

"Well, I'm glad that's under control. We've been friends for too long and needed to crush anything that could come between us. There *is* one more thing I wanted to say." She paused then blurted it out, "I've met someone!"

Angela choked on the Sierra Mist she had just swallowed while Nicki stared blankly as a brief wave of jealousy washed over her. "Why does everyone else deserve love except me," she thought bitterly. Once Angela had gained control of her breathing and her gag reflex was intact, Sissy continued.

"I met him after I took a tumble on the sidewalk, outside the Improv Theatre Sunday evening."

"Wait a minute," Angela interrupted. "You went to the Improv without inviting me? Then to add insult to injury, you met someone? I'm too through with you."

"Whatever Angela," Sissy waved her off.

"So what does he look like? Where does he work?" Nicki asked.

Sissy waited then leaned forward as though she were about to give away a trade secret. She began in a low voice. "Well, his name is Robert Douglas." She smiled, then with a slow deliberate pace continued while searching for the right words. "You guys know how I love a man with beautiful eyes." The women nodded. "So, of course I noticed those right away. His skin is latte in color with a ruddy undertone, which explains why people call him Red. He's average height, around five-nine maybe five-ten, well-built with square shoulders and a trim waist, clean-shaven and with a generous mouth that begs to be kissed."

"Girl, stop," Angela said then moaned afterwards.

Sissy added, "He has shoulder length, chestnut-brown dreadlocks."

"So when do we get to meet this dreamboat," teased Angela.

"Girl, please. We've only talked a few times." She didn't let on that the calls had taken place every day since they met.

"Well, I'm happy for you," Nicki smiled and gave her friend a hug.

"Thank you, baby girl."

"Ladies if you don't mind," Angela started, "I really need to go. I have two customers that are a handful. My first appointment is at nine in the morning and the other is at one in the afternoon. I must show their designs tomorrow so the company can stay on track regarding

completion of their remodeling. So I'll say aloha and goodnight."
Angela lifted her tray, stood up and walked to the trash bin.

"Translation, she's going home to watch another episode of the
original *Hawaii Five-O*" Sissy said.

"I forgot that she's in love with Steve McGarrett," Nicki added.
When Angela returned for her handbag, the two women started hum-
ming the theme song to the television show.

"Aren't you two just full of laughs? Don't be jealous of my man
Steve, Sissy. He can beat Marshall Matt Dillon from that old, dusty
Dodge City anytime."

"Oh yeah Sissy, you better watch out for Ms. Kitty. She may take you
down for messing with her man" Nicki added, trying her best to join
in the camaraderie as she grabbed her shoulder bag; but her mind was
still reeling from Sissy's news.

"And what are you laughing about," Sissy and Angela said while
looking in Nicki's direction.

"What?"

"We know how you feel about Perry Mason and Paul Drake the
investigator," Sissy reminded her.

"She's too tough," Angela chided. "She's playing two men in the
same office. You're some kind of woman. Della Street could take some
lessons from you."

Sissy and Angela gave each other a high five in between fits of
laughter. Nicki put on a brave face and smiled wanly as the trio walked
out of the restaurant and headed to their cars.

nine

Nicki was restless. There seemed to be a battle raging inside her head that she didn't want to deal with, and it wouldn't let her go. In fact it was beating the life out of her. She bolted upright in her bed while grappling for the light switch on the bedside lamp to her right. Her left hand flew over her eyes then slowly she removed it as they adjusted to the brightness.

Her head fell against the headboard as she looked around the room. Sissy's news had taken her breath away, and caused her to think seriously about her own life. She reached for the journal that had become a constant keeper of her thoughts and secrets. Opening it to the next available page she began writing,

I felt like a double barrel shotgun had been placed against my chest when Sissy announced that she'd found someone. This is crazy. All she had to do was fall flat on her face and out of nowhere, a man pops up, and a handsome one to boot. The only thing I've attracted was a cold and even that didn't stay around long.

Sissy deserves to find a good man after the heartaches she's gone through. I'm also proud of her for taking the time to put love on the back burner while she moved forward in her life. Now that's what I must do—move on. I'll call Sissy in the morning and discuss the possibility of going to the gym with her, at least until I feel comfortable going alone. I'm tired of feeling like a slug and looking so bad.

My clothes are too tight; my legs go numb when I sit on the toilet too long. This weight is like lead when I try to walk up a flight of

stairs. I'm thirty years old and I feel like I'm sixty. I don't know what
it's like to be beautiful anymore. What have I done to myself?

Nicki sighed and tossed the journal and ink pen on the nightstand. She turned off the lamp, slid back under the covers, and wondered...

—— ✾ ——

Angela was miffed that Cody wouldn't stay awake to talk to her. After all, it had been a week and a half since she'd last seen him. Granted, he called while working in Washington, D.C. and when he traveled to Fort Jackson in Columbia, South Carolina, but she missed his body and their intimate conversations. Angela considered herself in a relationship, after all they'd been dating since...she paused while mentally counting the months on her fingers, a year this October.

They exchanged the obvious romantic sentiments with each other, "love you!" and "wish you were here," and so forth but at thirty-five, Angela wanted more It was time to settle down and become grounded. When she purchased her home three years ago, she told her friends that she was, "coming down to earth." She wanted men to see her as mature and marriageable, someone to build a future with. Cody's soft snores distracted her thoughts and she looked in his direction. "This man is so fine," she thought while propping herself up on her left elbow so she could look down on him. Angela smiled as she gazed at his regulation haircut that enhanced the handsomeness of his square face and walnut-brown skin. She leaned over and kissed his eyelids while her cheek brushed his soft, black eyebrows. Cody's wide, dark brown eyes reminded her of a child in wonder. She continued trailing kisses over his normally clean-shaven face which was now sprouting a light stubble.

Angela's index finger traced his slender nose and soft cheeks, but all her attempts to awaken him hadn't worked. "I know I'm not losing my touch," she thought. She slid her mouth over his ripe lips and proceeded to nibble on his bottom lip to arouse some type of reaction.

He mumbled something incoherent then repositioned his six foot frame onto his left side. "Well that's just great," Angela hissed and jerked the bed sheet off her body.

She sat on the side of the bed, disgusted. "My hormones are raging out of control, and I can't get any relief from Sir Lancelot who's taking up the other side of my bed."

Angela stood up and started for the bathroom, kicking the clothes in her path that had landed on the floor a few hours earlier during their mad dash to the bed for some intense lovemaking. Now he reminded her of something from the frozen food section: an appealing package, but the contents needed to be thawed before use. In the dark room, which she knew all too well, she stepped on something bulky that caused her to lose her footing. Her hand landed on the wall for support. Thank goodness for the yoga classes that helped keep her balanced. She clicked on the bathroom light, causing the bedroom to fill with an eerie softness. It was Cody's wallet; she stooped and reached for the black and white leather item. Angela pulled the bathroom door closed just enough to allow a sliver of light into the bedroom without waking him.

She examined the wallet's unique pattern, an abstract photo of a man on a surf board as a wave approached him. Angela wistfully thought of what it would feel like to be on an island at this moment. Just as she flipped it over to close it, his driver's license caught her attention. Her eyes widened and she scrambled to the bathroom, closing the door and locking it.

Angela's breathing quickened. She closed her eyes and took several slow deep breaths. Once she had composed herself, she looked again at the license; the address on the card read Fort Leonard Wood, Missouri not Fort Riley, Kansas as he'd told her numerous times. Her stomach tightened when her eyes moved to the photo on the right side, opposite the license: a woman, Cody and twin boys smiled back at her. Her hands shook as she flipped to the next photo in the wallet. Cody stood proudly in his dress uniform as his arms encircled the same woman in a formal evening gown. The next picture showed the boys, much younger, the woman, and Cody posing together dressed in coordinating colors. She pulled the picture out to take a closer look and noticed writing on the back, "Christmas at the in-laws, 2002". Angela's hands trembled as she replaced the picture in the wallet, while a wave of nausea rose in her stomach.

"A family?" she said in disbelief. "He has a family." Her stomach clinched. She dropped the wallet and quickly turned on the cold water in the sink, splashing it wildly over her face. Once her breathing had calmed, Angela's first thought was to beat the life out of Cody with a baseball bat, but after some consideration, she settled on a more subtle approach. She took a few more deep breaths to gather her strength, picked up the wallet, turned out the bathroom light then opened the door. Just as she stepped out, Cody coughed a few times and she immediately froze in place like a statue. She could hear her heart beating in her ears and began to shake. He lazily shifted his position in bed and returned to a deep sleep.

She reached for the chenille robe on the back of the bathroom door, covered her naked frame then tied the sash. Tiptoeing from the bathroom into her bedroom, she paused briefly while clutching the wallet. Then she moved swiftly down the hallway, feeling like Tom Cruise trying to obtain classified information in some *Mission Impossible* movie. When she stepped into the kitchen her hands began to shake and once again she had to wait until she was under control.

Angela felt her way around the shadowy items in the kitchen, and after reaching the stove she clicked on the little light under the range hood. To her right was her 'whatever' drawer; she pulled it open. Inside were note pads, pencils, pens, paper clips and an assortment of odds and ends that had no home. Angela took out the first sheet of paper she touched along with a pencil and scribbled down the address from the driver's license, then stuffed the pencil and paper into the back of the kitchen drawer.

After she turned out the stove light, she retraced her steps back to her bedroom, paused, then proceeded once she heard his snoring. She made her way to the bathroom, and closed the door just enough to allow a weak beam of light to illumine the bedroom floor. Angela quickly located his pants and carefully placed the wallet in his back pocket, certain that he'd have no idea that it had fallen out. For once she was grateful for the three glasses of bourbon on the rocks that Cody usually had during dinner.

She left the jeans in a heap on the floor as she'd found them, turned out the bathroom light and returned to bed. Angela allowed the robe to fall from her shoulders onto the floor, gently climbed into bed and laid on her right side. She released the breath that she hadn't realized she'd been holding, letting out a deep sigh.

The man that she loved, that made her feel womanly and sexy was a liar. He was sucking up *her* air, messing up *her* sheets — all the while lying, telling her all the things she wanted, needed, and desired to hear.

She closed her eyes and then it happened. A steady stream of tears cascaded down her cheeks and onto the beautiful burgundy rose-patterned sheets that she used especially for Cody to welcome him back into her arms. Her best crystal wine glasses that had held Asti Spumante just a few hours ago sat empty on the bedside table, and for a brief moment she wanted nothing better than to crack those glasses over his thick skull! But not now, not yet; she was going to pay him back for the pain that he'd caused her.

"Phase one of my plan is complete," she thought. "In due time I'll execute phase two, my love," Angela murmured. "You just messed over the wrong girl Cody, and boy will you be sorry!" Once the flood of words ended, she cried herself to sleep.

After circling the lot more than once, Sissy carefully pulled her car into the coveted space in the second row to the right at "24/7-The Gym". Even on a Thursday evening the parking lot filled up fast. She glanced at her watch after stepping from her car, closed the door and quickened her steps to the entrance of the two story building. After scanning her membership card, Sissy entered the lounge area to await Nicki's arrival.

Five minutes later, her friend stepped timidly into the building and looked around. Sissy walked up to Nicki and gave her a quick hug.

"I'm so glad you made it," she said.

"I feel so out of place."

Sissy held up her hand. "Let's go." She walked until the scanner beeped Nicki's guest pass then slipped her arm around her friend's shoulders. Through the open areas above on the second level, Nicki noticed exercisers on bikes, rowing machines and a few treadmills. The noise in the building was almost deafening as machines competed with that of the overhead music and the television in the lobby.

"This place is huge," Nicki exclaimed as they turned into the dressing room to change clothes.

"Well, huge may be an overstatement," Sissy started, "but it *is* quite the place. After the workout we can have bite to eat in the café. Maybe you'll consider joining, and if so, a new member's director could speak to you."

Sissy wore a lilac T shirt and grape capri jogging pants while Nicki dressed in a black oversized shirt and black knit pants. She knew that in time as her friend's confidence increased her clothing choices would reflect it. Sissy tied the lace on her shoe and stood upright when she noticed the pensive look on Nicki's face and asked, "What's wrong?"

"I feel awkward. All those people out there are so much smaller than I am," she sighed.

"Nicki, I purposely had you meet me at eight o'clock for a reason; most of the after-work crowd have come and gone by now. We don't have to deal with the members with families nor the group exercise classes. Forgive me for being hard but here's another factor for you to consider: you're not the only large person this gym has seen. Other people have won that title, so get over yourself."

Nicki stared at her friend in disbelief. Never had she spoken to her in such a manner.

"Don't give me that bug-eyed look," Sissy continued. "All I'm saying is that you have to stop being afraid and making excuses. Either do this thing and get healthier or be happy with the skin you're in."

"Wow," Nicki sighed. "I guess I have been a little whinny huh?"

"A little?" Sissy snorted. "Girl, you just beat out a newborn baby hands down."

Nicki realized that she was being ridiculous and looked at Sissy, first with a smile and then with a deep laugh. The two walked out of the dressing room and headed to the second level to workout.

Once they stepped off the elevator, the area consisted of a sea of exercise equipment. Treadmills, elliptical machines, rowers, bikes and stair climbers were organized by row and style. Sissy pointed to the west side of the building, showing Nicki that there was even more equipment: Nautilus machines, free weights and a bare wood floor to place mats for stretching.

Sissy motioned Nicki toward an unoccupied row of treadmills immediately in front of them, and wisely selected the first two that were not located in front of the wall mirrors; so as to spare Nicki further embarrassment. Several flat screen televisions hung in the front of the room, each with a different program on it. Sissy helped Nicki set her machine for thirty minutes with a two point five walking speed, then stepped onto her own treadmill setting the speed high enough to challenge her yet still allow her to carry on a conversation with Nicki. Normally she would have her iTunes plugged in and cranked to her favorite songs while pushing through her hour workout, but decided to forgo it today. Nicki needed to feel comfortable in the gym to remain motivated.

They talked about work, the future trip to London and Paris and on how things were between Sissy and Robert. The machines were clocking the cool down period of the session when Sissy asked, "So how do you feel?"

"Not bad. It was easier than I'd imagined it to be. This place is great." The buzzer alarmed and the machine stopped as Nicki asked, "What's next?"

Sissy waved her hand. "Let's not overdo it. This was your first day so let your body adjust. You should come back two more times this week doing thirty minutes, and make sure you rest between each workout. Next week we can add another machine, maybe the elliptical. In the meantime let's grab a bite before the café closes and then we can pick up our clothes and leave."

They were finishing the last bite of their black bean veggie burritos when Nicki spoke. "Sissy, I can't thank you enough. The gym turned out to be better than I expected and I didn't feel as self-conscious as I thought I would."

"It's understandable." Sissy reached over and patted her hand. "Just imagine how I felt when I stepped in here alone, but now I come to the gym late in the evening and do my thing without any thought of who's in here. The building is staffed around the clock and the parking lot is well lit so I feel safe."

"I can tell that you are starting to tone up," Nicki complemented her.

"Thanks, baby girl. When we land in London I want to see my brother do a double take because he won't believe that it's me."

"Oh, you will definitely bring sexy back," Nicki said with a sly smile.

The girls high-fived one another then picked up their trays and dumped their trash. They returned to the locker room, gathered their clothes then stepped out the door of the gym to head home.

As Nicki sat in her car she replayed the past hour in her head. She'd felt like a hippo when she first entered the gym, but with Sissy's distractions she'd gradually dismissed that negative image as the thought of succeeding actually seemed within her grasp this time. The big question now was, would she have the courage to step foot in the building again—this time on her own?

ten

A week had passed since Angela discovered the information in Cody's wallet. She never let on during their times together that she was the wiser to his secret life, playing her part to the hilt. But inside she was miserable, crying at night alone in her bed when he wasn't around. She hadn't mentioned the incident to her friends, more out of embarrassment than anything else.

Somehow, someway she would make Cody pay for his deceit. He would look like a fool if she drove down to Fort. Leonard Wood and surprised his behind. Better yet, maybe she should have a little heart to heart with "The Mrs." She chuckled to herself as she played out scenarios in her head. "No man mess's over me and gets away with it," she said aloud. "I know the Bible says, 'vengeance is mine says the Lord,' but I'm going to help the Lord out and speed up the process."

After turning into the driveway of her new client's home, arriving fifteen minutes early, she knew she had to pull herself together before meeting Mrs. Carla Martinez. She and her husband were expanding the kitchen to include a sunken seating area to entertain guests while they prepared meals for various events. They'd also mentioned wanting a small guest bedroom off from the kitchen.

"It's probably for one of their buddies who gets a little tipsy and can't make it upstairs," Angela said aloud then quickly reprimanded herself for the thought.

She pulled out her cheat sheet to go over some of her clients' key points. The husband worked for the Saperstein Pharmaceutical Group in the new medications research department. Mrs. Martinez was the personal assistant to a Fortune 500 business owner. The couple has been married for fourteen years, a second go round for both. He has one son in medical school and another in his junior year at MIT. The wife has a thirty year old daughter in the Navy.

If Angela completed this project with the Bell Palmer Architect Group, it would provide great recognition for her. Even more, if they complete the project within the scheduled time frame without too many changes along the way, not only would she receive a nice bonus but the firm would offer her another design project.

With five minutes to go, Angela pulled out her Galaxy cellphone and texted an SOS to Nicki and Sissy to meet her at Anton's, 1610 Main Street at seven this evening. Talking to them would keep her sane while she continued to figure out the next step in her love life. She closed the phone and turned the ringer off dropping it into her tan leather tote bag.

"It's show time," she said aloud and stepped out of the car. She swept her hand over the single, breasted pinstripe suit then placed the tote over her left shoulder. Angela gripped the portfolio in her right hand, closed the car door, marched up to the home of Mr. and Mrs. John Martinez and rang the doorbell. In a low voice she recited her mantra, "I've got this, I own this, and I will win this."

Angela was sitting at the far end of the bar toying with her drink when Nicki and Sissy walked through the door. The hostess greeted them and the girls pointed to their friend. The woman stepped aside so they could make their way to her table.

"Man do you look like a pitiful sight or what?" Nicki commented as she pulled the chair out and settled in.

"What's wrong? Why the long face and the SOS?" Sissy persisted while scooting her chair in closer.

Angela took a deep swallow of her cosmopolitan, a bit heavy on the vodka, and then finally answered. "It's Cody. The flea bitten dog is married."

"Married?" the girls exclaimed.

"Yes, married!" she spat.

After giving the waitress her order for a Coca-Cola and a glass of water Nicki said, "Back this story up to the beginning and tell us how this happened?"

Angela explained the events of last week. When she finished, she noticed the look of disbelief on their faces.

"But you don't know for sure if that was his wife," Sissy said. "It could have been his sister and her children."

"I doubt that his sister is white with long blonde hair. The boys are biracial."

"That's messed up," Nicki sighed.

"It's more than that, it's…"

"Hey," Sissy exclaimed. "Watch your mouth, remember?"

"I know," Angela sighed. "Besides, I did all my cursing when you weren't around."

"So what are you going to do?" Nicki asked.

"I plan to drive to Fort Leonard Wood and check it out for myself."

"Did I hear you correctly?" Sissy asked nervously. "You're going there to confront Cody?"

"Yes ma'am. I want to see his stupid face as he tries to explain this other life of his."

"I don't think that's wise," exclaimed Sissy.

"I think you should," Nicki said defiantly. "And I'll go with you."

"You'd do that for me after the way I treated you?" Angela slurred as tears welled up in her eyes.

"To answer your question Angela, yes I'd do that. We're friends no matter what. This little game of Charades that Cody's playing is wrong, and he needs to be put in check."

"That's my girl!" Angela shouted and began to cry.

"How many of those things have you had?" Sissy questioned while pointing at the empty glass in Angel's hand.

"Three wonderful Cosmopolitans and some delightful appetizers," she answered, then turned her head and said, "So Nicki when should we go up there?"

"Friday, after five when I leave work. We can surprise the little family during their time together."

"Wait a minute," Sissy called out. "What's wrong with you Nicki? This isn't helping her and things like this can backfire."

"Let it," Angela said as she pounded her fist on the table. "I hope it blows him to smithereens." She slapped her hands and then opened them wide for effect. "He broke my heart and made me cry," she continued. "Now he must pay!"

"Preach it sister," Nicki encouraged her. "I'll bet he'll think twice before he does that again."

"I don't agree with either of you," Sissy huffed, "but we *are* the female version of the Three Musketeers, 'All for one and one for all.' Besides, someone will have to drive the getaway car, so count me in."

"Thank you Sissy, thank you Nicki," Angela said as tears coursed through her make-up and hung precariously on her chin.

"In the meantime, let's get you home." Sissy grabbed Angela's handbag as well as her own while she and Nicki took hold of Angela's arms and walked her to Sissy's car in the gravel parking lot. Once they had her seated and buckled in, Nicki took the car keys from Angela's purse and shut the door.

"I'll follow you to her house with her car and help to get her settled into bed then we can come back for my car." Nicki turned and took one step when Sissy stopped her.

"Going to Cody's house won't change anything, you know that?"

"I know but it's what she wants to do. Maybe Angela needs this whole thing to be real, not in her head but live and in living color. Sometimes we need that occasional slap in the face in order to move forward in our lives. Remember, you did that for me, so we need to be there for her."

"You are one smart soul sister Nicki." Sissy reached out and hugged her friend then stepped back.

"No, just a woman that understands the pain a man can cause. They dish it out then leave you to get over the mess they put you in." She smiled briefly then headed in the direction of Angela's car.

"Sissy," Debbie and Corinne called out in unison.

"Why is it that on the day that you have something planned, every-one wants you," Sissy muttered under her breath. Today she and the girls were to drive to Fort Leonard Wood. "Yeah, what's up?"

"Mickey's machine has a burning smell coming from it," Debbie blurted out.

"Yeah, we looked but can't find out what's causing it," Corinne added.

Sissy quickened her pace with the technicians trailing behind her. The alarm on the dialysis machine blared and a pungent smell filled Sissy's nostrils when she reached the equipment. "Grab another bag of saline," she shouted over her shoulder while filling a syringe with the small amount of fluid in the bag that presently hung on the I.V. pole above. Sissy grabbed the new bag from Debbie, switched it out with the current one and began the rinse back procedure, returning the blood to the patient.

"Corinne, write down these numbers as I call them out," she instructed. Debbie typed the patient's current vital signs into the com-puter. The technicians removed the broken dialysis machine from the area while Sissy pushed a replacement in its place.

"That's the one we tried to use this morning. The conductivity numbers remained high during the testing phase," Debbie informed her.

"I know but we haven't any other machines available. I'll place it in the rinse cycle for five or ten minutes then check if the levels will balance out. If that doesn't work, Mickey will have to return tomorrow to complete his treatment."

Twenty minutes later, the dialysis machine passed all the neces-sary tests allowing Sissy to restart Mickey's procedure. After instructing Debbie on documenting the completion of the patient's treatment and any other pertinent information, she yelled, "I'm outta here," and ran out the door.

"Are you sure you want to go through with this?" Sissy asked for the last time while they sat in her car. All the women had showered and changed out of their work clothes into casual attire and were now awaiting Angela's answer.

"Cody called, said he wouldn't be able to see me because he has a meeting with his commanding officer. So let's just finish this game out," she said in a deadpan voice.

Sissy turned on the ignition, checked her left and right side then carefully backed out of the driveway. Once she hit the street, she turned the wheel and down the road she went.

Fort Leonard Wood is located in the center of the state of Missouri in Pulaski County. The three to four hour drive passes through towns like Harrisonville, Garden City, Clinton and Warsaw.

Angela remained quiet, occasionally dozing off to sleep. Nicki sat in the back reading her steamy romance novel while Sissy sang along with the music on her Sirius radio system as the car sped along I-435 East for twelve miles, twisting and turning along state roads and highways until they reached MO-5/MO-7 finishing the drive down the back roads.

When they were forty-five minutes away their destination, Nicki put her book aside and reached over the front seats searching for the GPS. "Thank goodness for these little devices" she said after picking it up. She took out the yellow note paper with Cody's address that Angela had given her earlier. After setting the information into the machine she said, "Let's go skunk hunting."

"Look Nicki, we are *not* going into town with guns blazing as though we're hunting down an armed criminal."

"I know that Sissy," Nicki huffed.

"This is Angela's game so we'll play by her rules." Sissy looked to her right and noticed Angela staring out the window. She wasn't spewing obscenities or regaling them with scenarios of chaos and destruction as she had the night before. Her flat demeanor and quietness caused Sissy to be suspicious of what might happen once she faced Cody.

As they traveled through the suburban neighborhood, the girls noticed the two story homes that varied in styling. Some were brick, others were covered with grey, brown, or peach siding. The humid evening lured people from their homes to take walks. Some were alone, others were with friends, and then there was the occasional couple strolling along the path. The girls chuckled as dogs ran to sniff out each other, causing their owners to get tangled in their leashes. Occasionally they saw children running across manicured lawns. On the sidewalks, chatty women ran pushing expensive strollers as they strived to regain their pre-pregnancy figures. Angela took all this in, saddened at what might have been, but would not be. Sissy slowed the car as they made a right turn while the mechanical male voice said, "You will reach your destination in point four miles." She looked in Angela's direction, but said nothing. Her eyes returned to the road as the GPS said, "You have reached your destination on the right." All heads turned when Sissy stopped in front of the house at 2106 Martin Drive.

eleven

They gazed at the brick front two story home with moss green siding and white trim. Four large uniform hedges sat in front of the house. To the left of the front door was a small flower garden.

"That's Cody's car in the driveway," Angela said her voice barely audible. "I wonder how long he's been home." She looked at the white car parked in the open double garage. The personalized tag read, 'My Love.'

"Do you want us to come with you?" Nicki asked.

"No girls. This game is all mine," Angela said after taking a deep breath. She opened the door and paused when she heard the squeal of laughter. From the backyard of the house, two boys ran from the side to the front yard carrying what looked like Nerf water guns. They sprayed one another, laughing so hard that they fell on their knees. Once they recovered, the boys returned to the backyard.

"Angela, are you OK?" Sissy gently asked.

She nodded her head then stood on the grass, closed the door and turned toward the house. "I'm so stupid," Angela thought, each step felt as if her ankles were shackled with chains. Her breathing quickened when she reached the front door. Automatically her hand reached for the doorbell and pressed it. It was as if a lifetime had passed before the dark wood door opened. Cody blinked twice and then his eyes widened when he looked at the figure on the opposite side of the screen. He hastily stepped out onto the small concrete stoop pulling the doors closed behind him.

"What the hell are you doing here? How did you find out where I lived?" His words spewed out like molten lava from an active volcano.

"And hello to you too," she smirked.

He grabbed her arm and quickly walked her toward the driveway. The girls were watching from the car. His actions riled Nicki and she started for the door.

Sissy called out, "Where do you think you're going?"

"Did you see how he put his hands on her?"

"Leave it Nicki. Angela can take care of herself."

"He'd better not touch her again!" Nicki shouted then crossed her arms.

Cody and Angela stood in the driveway. "You have a lot of nerve asking *me* questions after you've lied to me for eleven months," Angela spat back.

"Look, this is not the time or the place to talk," he said. "Why don't you meet me…"

"Baby, dinner will be ready in ten minutes. Will you get the boys so they can clean up?" An angular, lithe, blonde stepped out of the door and joined them on the driveway. She was dressed in a pair of pink, cotton shorts and a matching halter top. Her feet were bare.

"Yeah sweetie, I'll get them," he said hurriedly.

"I'm sorry, I didn't realize you had company."

Cody licked his lips before answering. "Oh baby, this is Sargent Thomas from the base," he lied. "She had to inform me of some information my commanding officer forgot to mention."

"Hey," his wife replied in a muted, twang of a voice. She looked at Angela like an animal staking its prey. It's the stare a woman gives when she knows something's wrong.

"Hello," Angela responded in a steely tone. "By the way, I'm…"

"Brenda, go in the house. The boys and I will be there shortly."

The woman walked slowly to the front door, turned and looked Angela up and down before stepping inside the house. Cody's head spun around so fast that it could have snapped off its base. His eyes blazed when he spoke to Angela.

"Don't you ever come to my house again, do you understand me?"

"Punk," Angela's reedy voice began, "don't you dare threaten me." She jabbed her finger into his chest. "You tired, want-to-be player. I will march my fat butt to that door and tell your wife everything. You are such a liar. How could you do this to me? I don't deserve to be treated this way."

"Look Angela, it was fun while it lasted. You've got skills, not only with your job but in the bed, but do you honestly believe I would have someone like you in my life forever?"

"What?"

"You're out of shape, fat and would only get bigger over time. Do you think I would actually have you as my wife? Girl, you knew how to make me holler in bed but there's a limit to my taste for big girls, and baby you've reached it. So turn your fat butt around and go on back to your crib. And if you ever come by my house again tryin' to mess up my good thing, I will hurt you."

Before she realized what she was doing, she balled her right hand into a tight fist and with every ounce of strength inside of her Angela punched Cody hard across the jaw. The power of it all caused him to lose his balance as he fell against his car. She cursed him as she kicked him in the rib cage with her knee, then clawed his face with her nails. Just as she was about to strike him again, Nicki grabbed her arm and practically pushed her down the incline, and shoved Angela into the backseat of the car.

Nicki pulled her legs in, slammed the door and yelled at Sissy, "Punch it before they call the police!"

Sissy stepped on the accelerator and skidded away from the curb and down the street before Cody could make it to the sidewalk.

———— ∞∞∞ ————

They had reached the interstate when Sissy couldn't stand the silence any longer and turned on the radio. Ironically the song, "A Broken Heart" by Alexander O'Neill seeped through the car speakers swallowing up the quiet. Sissy cringed and turned the volume down. Her mind raced with questions she dared not ask. Instead she looked in the rearview mirror at Angela's distraught face.

Nicki's eyes met Sissy's briefly then Sissy broke the look and focused on the traffic ahead. Out of nowhere, what started as a sniffle, turned into a shriek. Before anyone knew what had happened, a pained, mournful cry poured out. Angela's hands hid her face and all that could be seen were her shoulders shaking in reaction to her sobs. Inwardly she admitted that Cody's words hurt, like an open wound that had been excised and left bare.

Sissy felt every bit of her anguish and blinked twice to hold back the tears. Nicki pulled several tissues from her purse and handed them to Angela. She took them and placed her head on Nicki's shoulder.

"Just cry it out," she said while patting Angela's hand.

"I know I looked like a fool back there," she said after blowing her nose. "More like an out of control idiot." She broke into another wave of tears.

"You were angry and hurt. Sometimes, those two things will make anyone crazy and out of control. Just ask some of the men behind bars for murder," Sissy said.

"Here's my question," Nicki began. "Do you regret the decision you made to come up here and face him?"

She lifted her head while wiping her eyes. Sissy noticed from the rearview mirror that they were swollen and red with mascara smeared below them.

Angela cleared her throat and said, "No Nicki, I don't regret it now that it's all over. The great Angela Thomas has been played, dumped and called fat all in one day. Cody said that he would have never married me because of my weight. I can't believe the arrogance of that man." She gave a strange laugh and continued. "He had the nerve to be mad at *me* because I disrupted his perfect world. What a jerk."

"Well, I'm sure he has some explaining to do to the little woman." Nicki started laughing and tried to stifle it but couldn't stop.

"What's so funny," Sissy asked.

"I was just thinking, I'm sure his wife was wondering why three, hefty black women wanted her man. If she had tried to do something to break up the fight between Angela and Cody, we would have snapped her in half like a toothpick and tossed her over our shoulders. Poor

Cody, he can't handle a strong woman. That's why Angela was able to slap him down."

"I hadn't realized I had hit him that hard until he fell."

"That's OK," Sissy said. "He needed a reality check. *Now* he knows that you don't put your hands on a woman. Nicki almost went after him when he grabbed your arm."

"Girl, I was going to knock him into next week," she huffed. The car erupted into laughter. Angela had swallowed too much air and started to cough. Nicki patted her back and they all began to settle down.

"Ladies, I want to thank you from the bottom of my heart. You are more than friends, you are my sisters and I love you so much."

"We love you too Angela," Sissy shouted.

"Yeah, even when you're being a snob," Nicki interjected.

"I can't help that," Angela said. "Well girls, I guess I *will* be joining you in that little club you began." A few fresh tears started again and she dabbed them away.

Nicki looked at her. "Do it because that's what you want Angela, not because Cody said all those things about you."

"Well if I'm going to London and Paris you know I can't allow you two old fogies to show me up." She blew her nose then continued. "Besides, with Cody out of the picture why should I stay behind while you and Sissy are having fun?"

"I'll have you to know Angela that I'm already on my way to being a sexy mama. I've been working out for a month, almost two, consistently," Sissy informed her.

"And I started exercising almost three weeks ago," Nicki added.

"Well you may have the jump on me but don't get too comfortable. I'll catch up," she joked. "In the meantime, it'll take a while for my broken heart to heal. I really cared for that skunk Cody."

"We know you did Angela," Nicki grabbed her friend's hand. "It's not easy and you'll cry over and over again. Then one day, you'll wake up and there won't be any need for tears."

"Amen!" Sissy shouted. "Oh, here's my song," she yelled out and turned up the volume until it was audible to everyone.

"I like this too," Nicki said and started singing.

"What is it?" Angela asked.

"'Happy' by Pharrell Williams," and she joined Nicki as they sang off key.

Angela leaned back and watched as her friends danced in their seats, bellowing out the catchy tune. Although her heart was breaking on the inside, one thing she knew for sure was that she was not alone. These two nuts; her friends, her sisters, would not leave her. No matter what may happen, they needed one another. Sissy called them the Three Musketeers, "All for one and one for all."

twelve

Robert rifled through a file folder then paused momentarily. "How long has it been since I spoke to Sissy," he wondered. "A week, maybe two." He tried to erase any thoughts of Sissy by concentrating on his work, but to no avail. As much as he wanted to avoid getting involved with another woman, this one would not leave him in peace.

He picked up the receiver of his desk phone and punched in her number. She picked up on the third ring.

"Hello?"

"Hi Sissy, it's Robert."

"Well, hello stranger." Her voice brightened. She had missed his phone calls but refused to be the desperate female that constantly called a guy.

Robert cleared his throat then continued. "Sissy, I apologize for the distance, for not calling sooner. The job has had its' share of pressures recently."

"Oh I understand that," she said. "The clinic has had five new patient admissions causing the evening shift to expand greatly."

"Well, I, um…" He couldn't figure out why he was so nervous then finally pushed through with his question.

"If you aren't busy this evening, I'd like to have dinner with you."

"I'm sorry Robert," her voice full of disappointment. "That would have been great but unfortunately, I'm working the late shift this evening. We won't finish until ten o'clock."

"I see," was all he could say.

Sissy quickly responded. "If you'd like, we could do so tomorrow night. I have the upcoming weekend off."

"That would be nice. My crew and I are working until noon. Maybe you and I could have an early supper then a movie afterwards if you're in the mood."

"Whatever you'd like." Sissy let out a slight giggle.

"Is something wrong?" he asked.

"Nothing's wrong," she reassured him. "I was just thinking, you must have had some southern breeding. You said 'supper'. Most people around this area say dinner no matter what time of day it is. When I worked in South Carolina, supper meant a meal around five in the evening, whereas dinner took place later, around eight p.m."

He smiled to himself then said, "You're a smart woman. I spent my summers in Barnwell, South Carolina with my grandparents. Now back to our date, let's say I pick you up around four o'clock. You think of where you'd like to dine as well as some movie choices."

"That'll work, I'll text my address to you in a few minutes."

"Thanks Sissy. I'm really looking forward to seeing you again." He meant it despite his fears.

"So am I. Well I'd better get back to work."

"Yeah, me too. Enjoy the rest of your day. Bye."

"Bye." Sissy disconnected the call and slid her cell phone into her uniform pocket. She stomped her feet and let out a slight yelp. "I have a date with Robert, I have a date with Robert," she sang to herself as she pushed open the door to the dialysis unit and returned to the clinic floor.

Angela's heart wasn't into her work today. She sat in her car in the parking lot at Lowes. It would be another fifteen minutes before the store opened, giving her mind too much time to think. She sipped her Tazo passion flavored tea and stared out the window at the cloudy sky. The Weather Channel said there would be a chance of rain today. Correction, a fifty percent chance that is. It really didn't matter to her either way.

She pressed her head against the headrest and closed her eyes. Three weeks had passed since the 'mission' had taken place. The emptiness and loss of Cody's presence hit her two days after the event while she was doing the laundry. In fact it happened while she ripped the sheets off of her bed, remembering the last time they'd made love. It was strange how simple acts of the day reminded you of the most profound things.

Angela reached into her pocket book and pulled out her phone. She felt like an idiot scrolling through her messages, rereading the old texts she had saved from Cody. Doing so only triggered the love she had felt for him.

> "Miss you so much. My dream is coming 2 pass 2 be with you. I want you 2 be happy because you worked hard and deserve it."
> "I'm just crazy 4 you and you'll never know how much."
> "Please b with me. Stay with me, let me love you."

Angela couldn't take reading his words any longer and pushed the delete button on the cell phone. When the question of deleting one or all the messages popped up, she chose the latter and watched as his lies disappeared from the screen. She turned off her phone completely and drifted off into a deep sleep to the accompaniment of the light drizzle that had just started its steady tap on the roof of her car.

Twenty minutes later, Angela awoke with a start, surprised that she had fallen asleep so suddenly and dreamt so intensely. She blinked a few times and looked around, the rain had stopped, and several cars now filled the lot since her arrival earlier. Opening the car door, she took a moment to drink in the fresh air. She picked up her handbag from the passenger seat, exited the car, and after locking it, walked towards the entrance of Lowes. "Petrichor," Angela suddenly whispered, "that's the funny word the meteorologist used this morning to describe the sweet scent of the air after a rain shower. I wonder if something like that can happen in a human soul," she murmured as a slight smile played on her lips.

———∞∞∞———

Nicki checked her watch. "Twelve-thirty already?" she whispered, then gathered the files on her desk. Her boss, Mr. Donald Stevens, had kept her extremely busy during the last two days. In fact, she had put in more hours during the last month as his personal assistant than in the previous six. Rumors had spread within the company that something big was in the works but she wouldn't believe it until told otherwise.

A meeting was scheduled for one-thirty to take place in the conference room with the top executives. Mr. Stevens mentioned that he needed her presence to take down the minutes. After placing the files in the completion box on the office assistant's desk, Nicki swung her purse over her shoulder and walked in the direction of the corporate cafeteria for a salad and fruit bowl.

She located an empty table near the cafeteria's large windows, placed her tray on the table, pulled out the chair and sat down. Once she was settled, Nicki reached inside her purse and pulled out a small, spiral notebook she used to jot down her meals. Sissy had taught her this simple trick to help her stay conscious of what she was eating at all times. She carefully measured out the packet of dressing before placing it on her salad.

It had been six weeks since she'd started working out and trying to change her eating habits a little at a time. As she ate, Nicki made a mental note of the things she would bring to work to stock her desk drawer: a couple of packets of nuts, those mini boxes of raisins and two or three bottles of protein shakes. She devoured the mixed green salad and suddenly realized she had gone too long since breakfast without having snacked on something to keep her cravings down. This was another lesson learned. Nicki swallowed a large glass of water, her fifth for the day, then disposed of the food tray and headed back to the office.

———✺———

Mr. Stevens stood up from the leather chair and looked down the mahogany conference table while taking a mental count of the attendees. He cleared his throat, called the meeting to order then took his seat.

"Ladies and gentlemen, I am happy to announce some wonderful news. We at Amalgamated Freight will enter into a partnership with Narrows Pears Shipping in Paris, France."

Amalgamated had held a wide and respected position in the shipping business for twenty-five years. A family-owned start up, Donald's father, Gary along with his brothers Thomas and Henry had created the company on a small amount of money and a lot of prayer. As Donald wistfully looked around the room, he knew his father would be pleased to see how his little business had grown. The group broke out in thunderous applause amid the rising murmur of voices. Mr. Stevens held up his hands to silence the room then continued.

"In a few months my presence will be required to sign papers, tour the plant and finalize the merger. In my absence Mr. Franklin Harris will assume leadership. Franklin, will you rise?" He paused as the portly, red-faced man stood and smiled. Mr. Stevens nodded at his colleague and Franklin resumed his seat.

"As my departure date approaches, I will send a reminder memo two days prior in case last minute questions or issues arise. I want to say thank you to everyone for doing such a fine job. Without your dedication, this merger would not be possible. To show my gratitude, this Wednesday, April 10, lunch will be catered by Andres' Confiserie Suisse who will also provide some of their fine deserts. This is a major celebration and I want to share it with all two hundred and fifty employees, so all directors, please spread the word to everyone in your department." Several heads bobbed up and down in recognition of his statement.

Mr. Stevens rose and said, "Once again, I thank you all, and now the meeting is adjourned." Laughter, chatter and handshakes took place immediately. The announcement had taken the group by surprise causing a wave of excitement. Nicki completed the last note of the minutes and stood to return to her desk to type them up when Mr. Stevens called out her name.

"Yes, sir?"

"Nicki, may I have a moment of your time?"

"Yes, Mr. Stevens." She resumed her seat as he walked over and closed the conference room doors. Nicki stared out the large pane of glass that looked out on the office lobby. She had never paid much attention to it until now. The walls were a cream color, and the hardwood floors gleamed as the sun spilled across them from the high, four-foot windows. The urban styled furniture…

"Nicki, I have a dilemma that I hope you can help me with," Mr. Stevens said as he settled in his seat, causing Nicki to cut short her observations as she turned to face him.

"I'll try, sir."

"As you've heard, I'll be flying to Paris in a few months. I'll need some help as this transition takes place. I know you requested vacation for October."

"Yes, I did. I wanted to make sure that there would be enough time to train someone to substitute in my absence."

"Have you found anyone?"

"Marge Becker, in the float pool, has agreed to do so. In fact, for two hours starting next week, she'll come in from eight to ten to start her training with me. She's smart and willing to come in every Monday to work."

"That's what I like about you Nicki, I can always count on you to be so efficient. That's why I know I'm right in asking this huge favor of you."

"Yes, sir, go ahead." Nicki knew one thing for sure. No matter what he said, her vacation was not up for negotiation.

"I was wondering if you wouldn't mind extending your stay in Paris a little longer to accompany me during this merger."

"What?" Nicki exclaimed. She knew that her hearing must have failed her.

"I've come to depend on your services a great deal and would be lost without you nearby to keep me, as you say, on point."

"Mr. Stevens, you want me?" I mean, I'm flattered but…"

"But what, Nicki?"

She paused, ashamed to say what was on her mind. She looked at her boss and said, "My weight. Wouldn't you be embarrassed for all those people, those men, to see me with you?"

"Nicki," he stopped while grappling for the right words. He could tell that the subject was a sensitive one for her. "I hired you for your excellent management and organizational skills. I won't lie, during the interview process I wondered if you'd have the stamina to keep up with the demands of the position. It was your confidence and the way you carried yourself that won me over. Two years later, I can still say that I made the right choice."

Nicki's eyes welled up as tears crested to the edge.

"Besides," he continued, "if you don't mind my saying, I've noticed some slight changes in your physical appearance. I'm proud of you. Keep up the good work. Now back to my question. Will you join me or not?"

"Of course I will," she squealed while brushing away the tears that covered her cheeks. She reached into her pants pocket and pulled a wadded tissue from it, then dried her face and blew her nose.

"We'll work out the details next week as I finalize travel dates."

"This is an honor Mr. Stevens. Thank you so much."

"No, thank you." He reached over and shook her hand. Afterwards he smiled then said, "Well, I don't know about you but I am ready to go home."

"But it's only three-thirty, sir," Nicki said after checking her watch.

"I'll let you in on a secret. I'm exhausted from all this happy news. I'm going home and will return tomorrow at eight in the morning, if not sooner. So you have my permission to use an hour or two of your vast amount of accumulated vacation time. Go home and cut loose." They both laughed as they walked out of the conference room. Mr. Stevens went ahead as she stopped to turn off the lights.

As Nicki proceeded down the corridor to her desk, she thought, "Why *shouldn't* I go home?" She put away her steno book, and then began shutting down her computer. "Today's a celebration, and a huge one at that." Nicki started to hum the theme song from the movie, *Footloose*. The computer screen went black and she gathered her purse and lunch tote. When she reached the office waiting room, she waved goodbye to Clarisse, the young secretary that sat at the crescent shaped reception desk. Nicki pushed through the glass doors and headed in the direction of the elevators.

As she sang aloud while pressing the down button, she did a little shimmy. Just as the doors opened, Kevin, the mail clerk, smiled as he caught Nicki in the act. She stepped in the elevator, slightly embarrassed, until she heard Kevin pick up the beat to the song. They finished out the chorus just as the elevator doors closed.

thirteen

Sissy tilted her head and studied the reflection in the full-length mirror: black dress slacks with matching suede pumps, long sleeved white blouse with wraparound ties secured in an ornate bow at the waist, and teardrop-shaped jet and crystal earrings twinkling on the earlobes. "Not bad," she whispered, winking at the reflection with satisfaction. "And now for the final touch," she reached for the silver and pink flask of "Chance" by Channel and spritzed her neck and chest, filling the room with the subtly sensual fragrance.

While replacing the bottle on the dresser, Sissy's eyes fell on the journal sitting on the nightstand; she hesitated, then moved quickly to the bed, picked up the journal, and jotted a quick note.

16:00

It's my first date, technically that is, with Robert. We hadn't spoken in two weeks and then all of a sudden he finally decided to call. I should be furious with him but for some strange reason I'm not. Everyone gets a little shaky before going forward with a new person. When he decided not to return my phone calls after I had tried to reach him for two days, I left the situation alone. Besides, I have a trip to London and Paris to prepare for and don't have time to obsess over some man's insecurities. Oh yeah, I checked the scale today — fifteen pounds lighter! I have a long way to go but this small dent in my size helps. I feel better and it makes my exercise program just a tad bit more tolerable.

She replaced the journal and ink pen on the nightstand and checked her watch. "Ten minutes before show time." Sissy picked up her small 1960s black, accordion styled purse and placed the few beauty items that she had laid on the bed inside, then walked into the hallway and started down the stairs. Just as she reached the bottom step, the doorbell rang. She paused for a moment, inhaled deeply then slowly counted to ten before continuing to the front door. Her hand shook slightly as she turned the knob and opened the door.

fourteen

"Welcome," she said, staring at the handsome figure standing before her.

"Thank you." He stepped across the threshold, then to the side while she closed the door. "Would you like to have a seat? I just need to make sure everything is locked and lights are turned on."

He looked at Sissy and couldn't believe he'd allowed so much time to pass before seeing her again. "Wow, you look great!" he complemented her as she walked him to the living room.

"And so do you. What's that cologne you're wearing?"

He paused for a moment to think and said, "'Red', by Polo."

"I like it."

He gave a low whistle when he entered the living room, "Man, I feel as if I've stepped into MGM's movie studio," he chuckled. "I would have never guessed you for a movie buff."

Sissy smiled while glancing around the room. "Yep, I've been one for as long as I can remember. It started in my teens with "The Late, Late Show" on television and grew from there. Make yourself comfortable and I'll be right back."

Robert admired the colorful movie posters with their beautiful frames. They looked as though a professional had hung them on the walls as various sizes played against each other to great effect. He smiled when his eyes landed on the walnut bookcase that housed an old movie projector with reels. Robert was surprised to find that one of the movie reels actually had a trail of film dangling from it! On the next shelf a set of broadcasting microphones sat proudly against a collection of books on the history of film making.

Ten minutes later Sissy rejoined him and asked, "Are you ready to go now?"

"Where in the world did you find these beauties?" he asked while pointing to the microphones.

"I love antiquing while traveling across America. There are so many out-of-the-way stores with buried treasure."

They began to walk to the front door when he turned back to face the foyer. "And what gave you the idea of making a collage with movie posters in this area?" his voice full of admiration.

"Oh this," Sissy pointed at the assemblage. "The married couple that owns the framing business that I use hung all of the posters you saw in the other room. One day, I explained to both of them my idea of creating a collage. The husband balked, but his wife thought it was a great idea and wanted in on the project. After all, I had given them a lot of business and because of it we'd become very close friends. So amid stacks of posters, we went to work hanging some, ripping others; layering them every which way for the effect we wanted. In fact it was her idea to camouflage the switch plates with the posters. We'd completed half the wall when her husband joined in. He admitted it was turning out better than he'd imagined and didn't want to miss out on the fun."

"He was right. Well, I guess we'd better go. I could stay here all evening and talk about your collections. I feel like I'm in a museum."

"I'll take that as a compliment," she said as they walked out the door.

Sissy couldn't seem to quiet the excitement that swirled like an impending storm within her. As they waited for a table she thought of Roberts's politeness and manners. Obviously his parents, especially his mother, had taught him well. It was refreshing to have a man hold the car door open for her as she slid in. Even when they arrived at the restaurant,

J. Gilberts, not only did he hold the door open for her, but also for the elderly couple that came in behind them. She took another whiff of his cologne while sighing inwardly. Sissy mused on the thrill she'd felt at seeing his almost six foot frame standing on the opposite side of the townhouse door. That erect, confident stance and his freckled, chestnut complexion almost caused her knees to buckle. She couldn't believe that broad-shouldered specimen was actually there for her. He looked like a fine piece of Godiva chocolate wrapped in a paper cup on display in the store's showcase.

She was shaken from her reverie when a chubby brunette hostess approached them and said, "I have a table for you if you'd like to follow me."

They both stood, Sissy moved forward as the woman escorted them to a booth. The soft lighting gave a sense of intimacy to the room without making one feel as though they were in a tunnel. Once they were seated and menus placed before them, the hostess excused herself allowing Robert to finally speak.

"I'm really glad to see you again."

"Same here," Sissy smiled.

"I'd forgotten how pretty you are."

"It's the lighting," she began. "It brings out the best in my complexion."

They both laughed then he shook his head. "All I know is that you're beautiful and I'm happy to be here with you."

She took a sip from her water glass and said, "Well, now it's my turn to speak."

"Oh?"

"You're looking rather sexy in those straight leg jeans. And that salmon colored dress shirt and skinny navy tie aren't bad at all. And to top it off," she paused and peeked under the table, then looked up again fixing her gaze on him, "those black Calvin Klein loafers make you look like you just stepped off the runway."

Robert couldn't control the rush of blood to his face while the widest smile ever came into view. He gulped down the glass of ice water and finally found his voice. "You really know how to make a man blush."

"Blush? You? No," Sissy teased.

"So, are you an underground fashion designer for Giorgio Armani or Dolce and Gabbana?

"I wish," she said winsomely. "I still dabble in making my own clothes from time to time. For example, my scrub tops for work, or summer dresses and, on occasion, clothes for my nieces and nephews."

"That's a nice talent to have." He paused when the waiter approached the table.

"Pardon me," a tense, lanky, dark blonde male said. He tried to hide whatever was bothering him. His voice remained professional. "My name's Alex and I will be your server tonight.

"And I'm Robert and this is Sissy. We'll be you're customers this evening."

The young man, caught off guard by Robert's comment, relaxed, and let out a deep laugh. "Well that's a first. I don't have many guests that introduce themselves. Could I start you off with a drink from the bar or something else?"

Robert nodded in Sissy's direction. "A cosmopolitan for me," she said.

"And I'll have a gin and tonic," Robert added. "I'd also like to order a shrimp cocktail as an appetizer."

"I'll get that started for you Sir, and your drinks will be here shortly." Robert nodded and turned his attention to Sissy. "Now back to what you were saying about the clothes you make."

"You're a nut, introducing us to the waiter," Sissy giggled then continued. "My youngest brother, William resides in London. My sister, Jessica, is married with a daughter, Misty who's five. My oldest brother, Maurice, is the father of two boys, Justin, one year old, and Jordan who is four. To help my married siblings, I make their little ones summer play clothes. They're easy, and the fabrics are so colorful and fun."

"A woman of many talents, I like that." Before she could answer, Alex returned with their drinks and the shrimp cocktail. They clicked their glasses in a toast and drank.

"And what about yourself," she asked picking up the conversation. "What holds your interest besides pretty women?" He lowered his glass and gave a half grin. Sissy caught a glimpse of a dimple in his left cheek.

"I'm a little different in that I like to study architecture. When I vacation, I'm that odd guy that goes on architectural tours like the ones they give in Chicago or New York. I also like watching the History Channel, second of course to all the sports channels."

"Of course," she responded.

"I shoot a few hoops twice a week with my buddies and at least three days a week I work out at the gym."

"No wonder his body's in such great shape," she thought.

"When it's possible, I like to take road trips out of state. Believe it or not, driving those long miles of asphalt is relaxing to me."

Alex returned to take their dinner orders. Sissy started, "I'll have the Twin Medallions with Yukon mashed potatoes, and grilled asparagus with rosemary demi."

Robert ordered next. "I think I'll try the eight ounce Cajun spiced pan roasted filet, poblano au gratin potatoes, and Shitake mushroom with port and sherry jus."

"Those are great choices," Alex said then turned and left the couple to their conversation.

While sipping their drinks, Robert cleared his throat before speaking.

"Sissy, I know it's a little early to ask but I was wondering if we could get together again. You're so comfortable to be with and I'm really enjoying your company."

She brightened. "I think that would be possible. I understand that your schedule is crazy like mine but, as the saying goes, "Anything worth having is worth the wait."

He gave her a quick wink. "I would like it very much and I must admit it's nice to shake the dust from my boots and relax with a pretty woman by my side." His index finger hovered over the back of her hand before it landed on her skin. With a back and forth motion, he stroked the soft flesh as though he were drawing the letter "Z"..

Sissy's toes instinctively curled inside her pumps. She sighed and said, "You are determined to take my breath away."

"I'd like to try," he admitted. His smile sent a tingle throughout her body. Before she could respond, Alex stepped forward with an over-sized tray on his shoulder. He popped open the stand he carried in the other hand and placed the tray upon it. After serving the pair, Alex asked if anything else was needed before stepping away. "Everything's perfect," the couple murmured, gazing into each other's eyes.

fifteen

"So Sissy, your work as a travel nurse puts you all over the map. Do you really like moving around like that, I mean every three months?"

"The original contracts are three months long but can be extended to four months or more. A lot of it depends on the work environment, if the company needs you or if you want to stay. Other times it's determined by the facilities budget. For the most part I enjoy it. I've learned a lot and met so many people along the way. I work as a dialysis nurse but there are also travel nurses that work in ICU, Medical-Surgical units and Pediatrics, for example."

"Wow, I would have never guessed."

"Believe it or not they even have doctors, as well as physical and respiratory therapists that travel."

"Get outta here," his voice was full of surprise. "But Sissy, don't you ever get lonely?"

"I'd be lying if I said I didn't. I usually feel the emptiness more around the holidays. When I'm on an assignment, the staff has their own family and friends to hang out with and I don't. Christmas is so special to me. Whenever there's a chance to travel near my home during the holidays, I try to take advantage of it. I love the decorating, preparing treats and everything that goes along with the festivities. It's fun to watch everyone's reaction when they stop by for a visit and see what I've done."

"Oh no," he said.

"What?"

"How many trees do you put up? I've watched those shows where people decorate the house, the yard, the town…"

"Whatever." She started laughing and knew he was right on all counts. When she finally got her breath she said, "I've decorated as many as sixteen trees."

"Sixteen?" he exclaimed and shook his head in disbelief. "Where did you put them?"

She hesitated for a moment. "Well, in the living room of course, and the laundry room, the bathroom, my bedroom…"

"The bathroom?" he questioned.

"It was a miniature tree."

"So not only are you a seamstress and a travel nurse, but you also hold the title to being the Christmas tree queen. I'm so honored to be in your presence." He bowed his head slightly.

"Thank you, thank you very much," Sissy used her best Elvis impersonation.

Robert looked at his watch. "Oh man, we've been in here for two hours. I've had so much fun with you that it doesn't feel like that much time has passed. Would you like some desert?"

"Something light would suit me just fine," she said.

"Let's get out of here. I've got just the place in mind." He reached into his back pocket for his wallet then picked up the folder that had been placed on the table some time ago. He slid several bills into the sleeve and waited for Alex's return.

───────

Sissy saw another side of Robert when they pulled into the parking lot of the Baskin & Robbins ice cream store. He behaved like a ten year old who had a dollar in his pocket that he couldn't wait to spend.

"This is one of the best places in town, thirty-one flavors to choose from! Rocky Road, Chocolate Chip and my all-time favorite, Reece's peanut butter cup. I love ice cream and it loves me back. Come on."

He quickly stepped out of the car and walked around to her side then opened her door.

"Yep" Sissy thought, "a true kid at heart."

Once inside the store, Robert wasted no time ordering when their turn came up. "One scoop of Chocolate Chip ice cream and make the other Cherries Jubilee, in a cup please." He turned to Sissy, "Order whatever you want," then stepped back and plunged into the cup that the clerk handed him. Sissy ordered a scoop of black walnut in a waffle cone.

"Do you need to go home right now?" Robert asked as they exited the shop.

"No, I'm off tomorrow. What's up?"

"I want to show you something if you don't mind."

"Lead on, Jasper," she joked.

Robert drove for thirty minutes, and then turned down a road that led to the old warehouse district. There was a large trucking convenience store, Mighty Mikes, which sat across the street, casting its bright beams of light into the area. Big rigs pulled into the parking lot in the back of the store as others were filling up their tanks before heading back on the road.

Robert parked at the construction site and turned off the engine. Heavy, galvanized chain linked fences surrounded the perimeter of the area. Orange cones were placed here and there as safety precautions. Large plastic coated banners hanging from the fences stated, "Think Safety" and "Use Caution. This is a Worksite, No Trespassing."

Robert stepped out of the car, ice cream cup in hand, and made his way over the ragged ground toward Sissy as she stepped out of the car and moved forward, placing her hands on the fence. Her fingers slipped through the diamond patterns as she inched closer and looked down at the massive hole in the ground. Suddenly she noticed several cylindrical concrete columns and steel beams. She stepped back and smiled.

"So, this is your work site?"

He nodded yes after filling his mouth with a spoonful of the slightly melted chocolate chip and cherry treat. Robert pointed at a grey and white trailer within the gates that served as his temporary office. A banner with a white background and bold, black lettering, waved in the light breeze. Sissy's eyes squinted to read the words in the dim light, R. Douglas Construction Firm.

Her attention returned to the deep pit, as she stared at the wood pillars and flat boards that reminded her of Tinker Toys. Huge, stagnate, greyish puddles of water rippled slightly in the man-made holes in front of her.

Robert swallowed the last of his ice cream and dumped the cup in the trash bin outside the gate. He walked over to a large sign on the outside of it and with his arms wide open said, "This is the future home of the Walter, Jones and Wendell law firm."

Sissy followed him around to the other side of the imposing chain link fence to an area that presented a better view of the work thus far. Metal rods lay in bundles on the torn ground. Piles of rich, brown earth sat in far off corners of the worksite while cranes and bulldozers that looked like dinosaurs, their mouths agape, silently awaited their next meal of dirt.

Robert stuck his hand through a section of the gate and pointed. "The ground floor will house a food court of four fast food restaurants, a Wells Fargo bank, and a Walgreen drug store. The law firm will occupy the whole fourth floor. There will be other businesses on the second and third floors."

"It sounds like you really study the companies that you build for." She admired his enthusiasm.

"The guys on my construction team tease me about it. They always ask why I get so involved."

"And you tell them what?" she asked.

"As a project manager, I'm responsible for the scheduling, manpower and money; which means, keep the budget in line. In the process of all of that, I develop a deep connection to each construction project. If I understand the use of a building, to envision the kind of clients that will use the services, it drives me to put forth my best all the time. It's no longer a building or a project, it has a purpose."

He took Sissy's hand and pointed out some of the equipment. "That machine over there that looks like it has teeth is an excavator, and that one is a boom lift. This big hole in the ground that you're looking at is really the first level of the parking garage."

"Oh wow!" Sissy moved closer to the fence. She grabbed hold and pressed her face against the chain links.

"Later," Robert continued, "we'll backfill this area and shore it up for the second level parking."

"So how many people do you have working for you?"

"I have a core team of twenty guys but that doesn't include the subcontractors."

"Subcontractors?" she asked.

"Those are the guys that, for example, put in the carpeting, or do the painting. We have a group called MEP's, mechanical, electrical and plumbing. On a construction site, the electrical guys in that group determine how much electrical power is needed for a project. They also determine the size of the service and the load. Each subcontractor estimates what size labor force they'll need, and makes adjustments if necessary. If you visit during the day you can actually see what goes on. It's fun to look at a draft and then see the actual construction."

Sissy stepped next to him and placed a kiss on his cheek. "I would enjoy that. You're not only a handsome, fun guy to be with, but also an energetic and caring person. In other words, I like you," she smiled " and I've really enjoyed this evening."

The rail yard across the street and to the right became active as the safety arms dropped into position interrupting the traffic on each side of the tracks. A horn bellowed and the sensation of the BNSA train with tankers and coal cars roared by, causing the ground to rumble beneath their feet.

Robert turned to face Sissy then slowly leaned in, pausing for a moment. When he sensed that it was safe, he pressed his mouth to hers. Sissy's lips parted and welcomed him to come further. His moan aroused sensations throughout her body that she had suppressed for much too long. His arms enveloped her as though he were afraid she would run away.

Sissy felt as though she were walking on hot coals. When he pulled back he said, "I hope that wasn't too forward. I've wanted to kiss you all night."

"Quiet," she said gently while placing a finger across his mouth. "I want to taste that chocolate chip ice cream on your lips again."

He chuckled then said, "Oh, let me help you with that," and pulled her closer. He kissed her more intensely than before, and he didn't care who might be watching.

sixteen

Nicki stared out of her apartment window. Thick clouds darkened the skies blocking out any chance of the sun coming through. As her hands reached out and touched the window pane, she shivered from its coolness. Instinctively she jerked them away and quickly wrapped her arms around her body.

She looked down at the scattering of leaves that covered the lawn below in colors of gold, burgundy, and dark brown. It was October, in two weeks Halloween's long tenuous fingers would bring with it children in costumes looking for treats.

The unwelcome approach of old man winter caused her to think of Sissy and her battle with seasonal affective disorder, SAD. Nicki had read that it affected hundreds of Americans during this time of the year. It seemed that the older her friend got, the more difficult it became for her to deal with the illness. Her moods at times were dark and her behavior flat and uncaring. Nicki had spoken to Sissy, asking if she thought her weight also triggered the depression she felt.

"I know this extra baggage doesn't help the situation." Sissy tried to laugh it off. "It's a struggle just to go to the gym," her voice full of despair.

"Is there anything I can do to help?" Nicki felt deep concern for her friend.

"No, but thanks anyway. Eventually it'll run its course and I'll be fine," then she quickly changed the subject.

Nicki understood her friend's battle with depression because of suffering through bouts of it herself after she and Michael had broken up. That's why she made a point of checking on her at least every two or three days.

Nicki walked away from the window and returned to the clothes piled on the ironing board. She moved them to a small table in the living room, plugged in the classic metal steam iron and placed the spray bottle on the opposite end. As she shook out a navy blue shirt-waist dress, placing it on the ironing board, she recalled how Sissy and Angela teased her about her 'old fashioned' ways. What was wrong with someone ironing their clothes? Nicki found it to be very relaxing and enjoyed the look of her garments afterward. In a way, it was a type of therapy for her. Ironing clothes was no different from people who found pleasure in cleaning a home, baking or knitting. What might seem like work to one brought comfort to another. It gave Nicki a sense of pride in completing such a minuscule task. At the job some of her co-workers would come to work in wrinkled clothes that made them look so unkempt, with the excuse that, "The dryer cycle is enough ironing for me."

As the steam hissed and rolled out from the top and sides of the iron while she smoothed away the wrinkles, Nicki reminisced about the weekends spent at her grandparents' home and the white, tattered basket of brightly colored laundry that needed to be done before the day's end. Grandma Jenkins loved hanging clothes on the line. She told Nicki numerous times, "I don't care about those fancy clothes dryers. My clothes are fresher and my sheets whiter when I bring them in from outside."

Nicki felt that because of her weight issues it was even more impor-tant to look and smell good. She made it a point to shower every day, cleaning between the folds of flesh that made her feel like Jabba the Hutt, the character from the movie, *Star Wars*. Nicki also found it nec-essary to wear makeup to deflect any attention from her body. People had a tendency to comment on how attractive her facial features were while avoiding the obvious.

She never wore over the top or dramatic makeup like Angela, instead Nicki chose to keep her look soft and simple with foundation, face powder, blush, mascara and lipstick. On occasion when the girls wanted to dress up and go out she would add eye shadow for more depth. She refused to give anyone at her job an excuse to say that she was fat and slovenly. If she looked presentable and smelled nice, she felt that it would deflect any gossip about her weight.

———⊗⊗⊗———

Tired and disgusted, Sissy hung her coat in the hall closet then tossed her keys on the outside of the staircase railing. She walked to the kitchen and looked at the wall clock.

"It's seven-thirty, too late for me to eat anything heavy." Opening the refrigerator, she searched its contents, finally pulling out a clear, plastic bowl with a blue top.

"Well I guess this Southwest Chipotle salad and a protein drink will have to be it for tonight," she said aloud while opening the nearby drawer and pulling out a fork then placing everything on the kitchen table. After retrieving her diary and ink pen from the living room, Sissy returned to the kitchen, plopped down in a chair, and began writing as she filled her mouth with salad.

> 8 p.m.-Went to the gym, for all the good it does me. I feel like I'm wasting my time there, but deep down I know it's not true. I'm just mad. I saw this handsome creature with defined arms, chest and legs. His butt wasn't bad either. When I casually walked in front of his treadmill, I thought I would pass out from shock. Oh, my goodness he was so fine! I had to check my mouth to be sure there wasn't any drool running down my chin. Seeing him made me realize I had been out of the dating game much too long. I smiled while walking past his machine and he nodded in acknowledgement then punched the buttons on the machine and began to run faster. Maybe that was his interpretation of running away from me. I chose a treadmill two rows behind him and chugged along while imagining he was all mine.
>
> I know that Robert and I have started seeing each other but sometimes a girl just wants validation from other men that she's

attractive. I can't believe I've allowed my weight to get so out of hand. Although I'm doing something about it, the results are slow in coming.

Sissy closed the journal, gathered her dishes, and left them in the sink; she didn't feel up to washing them, in fact she could hardly make it up the stairs to her bedroom. The depression that she suffered from at this time of the year surrounded her like a heavy cloak. The only thing that she wanted was a warm shower and a soft bed.

seventeen

The cold winds of fall caused tree branches to scratch and bang against Angela's living room window on a late Saturday evening. Nicki, worried about Sissy's continuing depression, had called earlier in the week and suggested that an intervention might be necessary. It was Angela's idea to throw an impromptu "Bellyacher's Bash" at her place. "It'll give everyone a chance to moan and groan about life without Sissy feeling self-conscious," she explained to Nicki. When she opened the front door to let her friends enter, dried leaves swirled and danced on the stoop. A few leaped over the threshold, landing on the linoleum in the entry but were crushed underfoot as the girls scurried inside to escape the cold.

Dressed in their most comfortable jogging pants and T-shirts, Nicki and Sissy joined their friend in the living room, laden with containers of shrimp fried rice, sweet and sour shrimp, beef and broccoli over rice, and egg rolls.

Two hours later, after indulging in their late night feast, Nicki complained, "I feel like a fat rat with one tooth," as she slouched into the sofa.

"OK, where are the traps?" Angela called out. "We have rodents in the house!"

Nicki reached for a throw pillow and pitched it at Angela who yelled out, "You missed me," while jumping to her left.

"Both of you have lost your minds." Sissy said. "I've already lost mine," her voice sounded so hopeless.

Angela moved to the loveseat, folding her legs underneath her as she sat. Nicki repositioned her frame on the sofa to listen. They could tell their friend needed to vent.

"Baby, what's going on?" Angela asked with sincerity and concern.

"I don't know. I feel as though I've stepped into a pit of quicksand and I'm sinking fast. I can't seem to stop this... feeling." Suddenly, tears cascaded down her face as she let out a deep sigh.

"Have you started your medication, the Cita-, oh, I can't remember the name of it," Nicki said out of frustration.

"Citalopram," Sissy clarified for her. "Yes I did, but I guess I started too late in the season."

"Well the important thing is that you're taking it now," Angela insisted.

"Yeah, I know."

"Now, don't take this the wrong way Sissy, but this happens to you every year around this time. Why didn't you start your meds sooner?"

"Angela, you have all the warmth of a wildebeest," Nicki said.

Sissy smiled sadly then answered the question. "I thought I could go at least one year without them. But you're right for once, Angela. I know that my serotonin levels, a chemical in the brain that affects mood, drops because of the reduced sunshine."

"And don't forget about the melatonin that gets thrown off because of the season."

"When did you become so knowledgeable about this stuff, Missy?" Nicki asked.

"My aunt on my daddy's side of the family confided in me last year that she suffers from the same thing. She uses medication and light therapy," she added.

"Oh," Nicki answered meekly.

"Girls," Sissy interjected, "thank you for your concern. I'll be fine once the medicine settles into my system. Just bear with me as I go through this tidal wave of emotions." All of a sudden tears trickled down her cheeks again. Nicki and Angela walked over, each taking a seat on the arms of Sissy's chair. As they leaned in to hug her, the two women fell into Sissy's lap, followed by the sound of a loud "thunk" that echoed in the room.

Angela tumbled to the floor while holding her head. Nicki followed afterward, yelling, "Watch out."

The sight of her two friends at her feet like heaps of dirty laundry moved Sissy from tears to a low snicker. Before she knew it, the loudest, deepest laugh gushed from her belly outward. Nicki and Angela looked at each other and shook their heads then turned and stared at Sissy.

"Glad to know that our pain could take you out of yours," Angela commented as she pushed herself upright.

"I'm sorry," Sissy guffawed. "You have to admit that watching you two grown women falling all over each other was a sight."

The two stood up and gave their friend a kiss on each cheek. "How about a movie?" Angela called out over her shoulder as she limped towards the television.

"Oh, what about the *Bucket List?*" Nicki yelled out.

"Since I'm the ill one, my movie choice is, *Brief Encounter.*"

"Ding," Angela pretended to be a bell. "*Brief Encounter* it is." She rummaged through her collection of DVD's and pulled out the case.

"I'll get the Kleenex," Nicki said. "I know that I'll be slingin' some snot and tears so I might as well be prepared."

"You're so nasty," Angela exclaimed while twisting up her nose.

"Whatever," Nicki said as she returned with the box in her hand. She settled onto the sofa pulling her legs under her body.

"I'll make the popcorn," Angela volunteered after hitting play on the remote control. "I have Jiffy Pop, the one that cooks on top of the stove. When I was a little girl, I used to think it was magic the way the foil in the pan went from being flat to the size of a bouffant hairdo."

"Girl, you're so silly. In the meantime, I'm going to curl up in this chair and enjoy the movie," Sissy said. She could feel the puffiness in her eyes from all the tears she had shed but it made no difference to her. At this moment in time the only thing that mattered was being in the company of the two people that she loved, and who cared so very much about her. She knew that her depression had to run its course. Sissy watched as the two women she called her friends rushed in and out of the living room. They felt more like sisters instead of friends. Right here and right now she felt loved and protected because of them. With time, she knew she would make it. Angela and Nicki would see that she did.

Nicki rounded the corner and stepped into the kitchen stopping in front of the stove for another pan of popcorn. Angela grabbed her arm before she could leave. "I'm worried about her," she confessed.

"She'll be fine."

"Are you sure?"

"Of course! What's worrying you?"

"I'll lose my mind if anything happens to that girl." Angela said. "My aunt, the one I was telling you guys about, almost committed suicide. My uncle took her to the doctor and that's when they diagnosed her with depression. I just hope it doesn't happen to me," she sighed.

"Ms. Thang, you don't have to worry about that. You're too evil!

"Whatever!"

"We better go." Nicki gave Angela a big hug. "Remember we're The Three Musketeers."

"You know it girl." Angela turned off the kitchen light as they headed toward the living room to join their friend.

eighteen

It was a brisk Halloween night, just as you'd expect this time of the year, and Sissy was adding the finishing touches to her costume. Two weeks earlier, she'd been mildly surprised by Robert's insistence that they attend a party given by one of his longtime subcontractors.

"He's a great guy," Robert began. "His name's Albert Strong and his parties are always a big hit. He's rented a club, hired security, contracted a caterer, and booked one of the best DJs in town; he really lays down some great tracks. Besides, after telling me about your struggle with seasonal depression, I felt it was my duty to keep you from being alone so much," he admitted, gently planting a kiss on her lips.

Now the day had finally arrived. She felt that she owed it to him to at least try since he had been so supportive during her blue moods. Maybe going out and having some fun would be a better diversion than eating everything in the refrigerator.

This would be Sissy's first grown-up Halloween party ever. Truth be told, she really enjoyed staying at home, passing out treats to all the goblins, dancers, and cartoon characters that would ring her doorbell. She would get into the spirit of the season and dress as an escaped convict, a distressed housewife or, her best one yet, a houseplant. The children and parents alike always commented on her yard decorations and get-ups.

When she shared the news about the party with Nicki and Angela, they thought it was great and began to come up with ideas for her costume. Sissy thought it would be fun too, until now.

"Hey, aren't you dressed yet," Nicki yelled up the staircase. "You know Robert will be here soon."

"Cool it chick. I'll be down in a minute."

"And you're missing the part in the movie where the creature is about to make his move."

"I've seen *The Creature from the Black Lagoon* a million times already. I think I could act out all the scenes," Sissy said as she started down the staircase.

"Nicki, I really appreciate you passing out the candy and stuff to the kids. I didn't want to waste fifty dollars' worth of treats."

Nicki swallowed the pretzel she was chewing while leaning against the wall in the hallway. "I got this girl. Besides, I didn't have anything to do this evening, so why not? Your plasma television is better than mine and I get to watch the monster marathon too. Shoot yeah, I got this."

Sissy was laughing at her friend when the doorbell rang.

"Coming," Nicki sang out. "It's probably more little monsters. The word's out that you have the best stash in the neighborhood," she said, admiring Sissy's costume.

Nicki yanked the door open and said, "Trick or ..."

"Treat?" a deep voice responded.

"Hey, we've got Hitchcock in the house," Nicki called over her shoulder. She opened the door wider as their mystery guest stepped in.

Sissy squealed drawing her hand to her mouth. "You look great! I didn't know Alfred Hitchcock was so handsome."

"Good evening," Robert said in the same breathless, paused voice as the Master of Suspense. He stepped further into the hallway as Nicki inched by to fill the treat bags of the children coming towards the house.

Robert looked Sissy over, his eyebrows arching upward. "You make a fetching Tippi Hedren." He stopped suddenly and said, "Where did you, how did you..."

"So you like my furry creatures?" she said referring to the fake birds on her shoulders. He continued to circle her while admiring the blonde wig that was fixed in a French twist. One bird, a blue jay, sat perched toward the front and center of her hair. He found another, a sparrow, to the right of her ear. He pulled her into his arms. "You look so tempting my dear," he whispered.

"Oh Alfred," she purred.

"I want to attack you like your feathered friends." He made a deep growl and swooped in for a soft, succulent kiss.

"Excuse me Alfred and Tippi, but this is a G-rated event so you two need to go." Nicki pretended to be indignant as she pointed to the front door.

The two turned their heads in her direction. "I guess I'm being kicked out of my own house," Sissy snorted as she righted herself then walked over to the chest in the hallway and gathered her purse and shawl.

Robert grabbed her free hand. "My lady, our chariot awaits."

The two stepped out the door as Nicki shouted, "Goodbye sweet prince and hot chick. Enjoy yourself and don't do anything that I wouldn't do."

"If that's the case," Robert shouted back, "you'd better call the fire department, 'cause I'm gonna' burn that place down with my good looks and charm."

"Oh brother," Sissy said as she jerked his hand. "Let's go Big Poppa!"

When they arrived at their destination, Robert kissed Sissy once more, allowing his touch to linger a few extra seconds on her lips, before exiting the car and walking around to the other side to help her out. As he opened the door, she was tempted to pull him on top of her. "Down girl," she thought to herself. The cold air that rushed in from outside quickly calmed the rising heat that Robert's kiss had stirred.

After waiting fifteen minutes in the long line outside, they finally stepped into the entrance of the club, Inspire. The music's vibrations bumped and thumped throughout the building, entering into the muscles of the dancers that gyrated, slithered and grinded into each other on the dance floor. Robert instinctively reached for Sissy's hand as they merged through the crowd. The strobe lights gave the dance figures an eerie look, like modern art come to life.

Sissy watched as Frankenstein and Dracula walked past them. A willowy figure standing in a half lit corner, dressed like Wonder Woman, did not do justice to the costume. "The real Wonder Woman would slap that chick," Sissy thought, then giggled.

They pushed through the crowd and almost collided with a waitress carrying a tray full of an assortment of drinks.

"Ooh, that was close," Robert shouted over the din of music and voices while steering her onto the dance floor.

"Hey, check out Alfred Hitchcock," a pudgy, red faced sheriff said to his girlfriend that trailed behind him. Roberts's eyebrows shot up when he noticed that she showed more than enough butt cheek hanging out of her Daisy Duke shorts, to the great enjoyment of the guys that stood at the bar railing gawking in her direction.

Robert and Sissy stepped onto the dance floor as the song, "Can't You See" by the deep voiced crooner, Barry White, poured from the speakers.

To Sissy's surprise, Robert broke out into a two-step dance routine. He took her hand into his, sliding his fingers down to her fingertips and sending chills throughout her body as he twirled and dipped her into a spin that caused the other dancers to pause and form a semi-circle around the pair. The couple mouthed the words to the song as they continued to display their moves on the floor, ending with big bow and applause from the delighted crowd once the music ended. Some of the other dancers walked over to Robert and Sissy and commented on how much they enjoyed the impromptu show.

"Wow," she said breathlessly. "I didn't know you had moves like that."

"There's a lot you don't know about me, lady," he answered then took the handkerchief from his breast pocket and dabbed at the moisture that had formed on her face. "Stick with me kid and I'll show you a thing or two." He gave her nose a quick peck then led her off the dance floor.

If Sissy had felt the least bit apprehensive, it was gone now. They mingled with the crowd, and danced more times than she could ever remember doing in her life. Each was asked to dance with other people and they were happy to oblige but found the greatest pleasure when they were back in each other's arms.

A couple of times, Sissy collided with a few overzealous drinkers. "Thank goodness," she thought, "that Albert had the foresight to hire enough security guards and a few off-duty police officers for the party."

When anyone showed signs of rudeness or strange behavior, they were escorted to the lounge area to calm down, drink some coffee and get themselves together. If that didn't suffice, a Care Cab was called and the party was over for the offender.

An hour later, Robert shouted over the sounds of, "U Don't Have to Call" by Usher, "Are you ready to grab a bite from the buffet?"

"Sure! All this dancing has burned a few calories," she joked while patting her stomach.

"Let's go baby," Robert said as he grabbed her hand and led the way.

Just as they were about to cross the threshold to the buffet room, Robert stopped abruptly causing Sissy to collide into him.

"Robert?" a husky, female voice asked.

"Candice?" His tone sounded more like a question than an answer. Peering over his left shoulder, Sissy's eyes widened at the character that stood before him.

nineteen

"Well hello, stranger," the voice shouted over the noise. The action all around them seemed to come to a halt as Robert stood in the passageway staring at the female in front of him blocking his path to the buffet table.

The five foot five figure in stilettos filled out a form fitting, bluish-black gown with a plunging neckline and a hem that trailed on the floor. She reminded Sissy of the character, Elvira, Mistress of the Dark, who hosted the late, late movies she watched as a teenager.

Sissy couldn't help but to stare at the large set of tatas that spilled forward with a little help from Victoria's Secret. A silver necklace in the shape of a bat rested comfortably upon them. Long locks of raven black hair cascaded down her back and shoulders as a whisper of bangs drew attention to her face.

Candice's large eyes, heavily made up with shadow and kohl, were transfixed on Robert as she pursed her scarlet colored lips seductively and crinkled her nose. Her stance exuded confidence, knowing that she looked great as one leg slipped through a slit in the gown that traveled up her thigh. Sissy began to feel uncomfortable as she became keenly aware of her weight.

"Excuse us," a robust voiced male bellowed from a wolf costume while pulling a woman dressed in a skimpy Little Red Riding Hood outfit behind him. Candice, Robert and Sissy, stepped aside allowing the crowd that had gathered behind them to pass.

Afterward, Robert collected his senses and quickly made the proper introductions.

"Sissy, this is Candice Rice. Candice, Sissy Bakersfield." Each woman gave a curt nod while silently eyeballing the other.

"Nice costumes," Candice said, her scarlet lips still upturned.

"Thanks," Robert quickly answered. "Well if you'll excuse us, we were about to check out the buffet table. You know Albert can lay out some food. He really outdid himself this year with the separate, pay as you go sea food section. Shrimp, clams and crab legs, here I come."

Sissy noticed a tangible nervous energy coming from Robert. He was trying his best to depart from the presence of the beautiful, dark skinned woman that made him very uncomfortable. Just as he made a move forward, Candice stepped in front of him to block his way.

"I need to discuss something with you. Could you call me tomorrow? It's important." She stared into his eyes until he nodded in agreement.

Candice scarcely moved her head to look in Sissy's direction before saying, "Good luck." She turned on her black stilettos and walked away.

"Wow," Sissy uttered.

Robert gave her hand a tug. "Let's go check out the food."

Sissy stepped up to the salad and appetizers and mechanically placed a few carrot and celery sticks on her plate. She picked up a chunk of cauliflower and sank her teeth into it, chewing on the vegetable like a bite stick to keep her from saying a few choice words that she had to hold back. "Down girl," she thought to herself as she tore into the celery stick, no longer feeling the giddiness that had engulfed her earlier in the evening. There were questions to be answered, but this was not the time or the place to discuss the matter.

———— ⤫ ————

Sissy noticed Robert by the sea food buffet but chose not to wait for him. She walked out to the main room and leaned against a pillar while she finished off the last of her steak kabob and tossed the paper plate into the nearby trash can. She was surprised at how much food she had eaten, but then again that was the only way she could keep from cussin' Robert out. If she were honest with herself, she had to admit that the evening was a blast until Ms. Sultry appeared.

Sissy gazed at the dance floor and noticed that the lights were dimmed as the music took on a sexy mood. "Come Away with Me" by Norah Jones, prodded all the lovers, and those seeking someone to love, to sway and cuddle on the dance floor under the guise of darkness. She watched as one of the couples closest to her displayed an erotic scene of passion so intense that Sissy looked around for something to fan herself with. It was obvious that the X-rated pair were oblivious to their surroundings.

A pair of hands encircled Sissy's waist startling her as she jerked around to find Robert looking back at her.

"Hey baby, you want one last turn before we go?" he whispered in her ear. "I have a heavy work load in the morning and need to head out soon."

Unable to speak, she nodded in agreement as they joined the other dancers on the floor. When Robert pulled her close to his chest, he noticed the tenseness in her body. He brought his lips close to hers and said, "We'll talk about what took place later. Right now I need you to loosen up and dance with me."

He took the tip of his tongue and traced her lips until they parted, allowing him to enter and kiss her passionately to the sounds of "At Last" by Etta James.

His hands caressed the center of her back as his lips moved to her neck. He nuzzled his face into the softest spot he could find. Try as she might to be mad at him, Sissy felt as if she were standing under a soft, shower of warm water, melting her anger away. His body felt protective and desirable as the scent of his cologne drifted past her nostrils and awakened her senses.

Sissy closed her eyes and moved with the sway of his body wanting to go wherever he wanted to take her. Her eyes drifted open as though she had awakened from a long nap. When her vision finally adjusted to the people outside the dance floor, she noticed Elvira aka Candice staring in her direction. Sissy righted her head just as the woman raised her wine glass to her in a mock toast and took a long drink.

"I think it's time to go," Sissy said abruptly, breaking free of Robert.

"What?" he said, stumbling slightly after she pulled away and walked off the dance floor.

"The Mistress of the Dark is staring us down," she yelled over her shoulder.

Quickly he looked up just as Candice took her right hand and trailed it seductively over her left breast while glaring in his direction.

Robert shook his head and let out a deep sigh. He stepped off the dance floor, walked up to Candice and said, "Not cool. Not cool at all."

He followed Sissy down the hallway that led to the exit. In the background the last song he heard, "Nowhere to Run" by Martha Reeves and the Vandellas echoed his sentiments as he fought to keep pace with Sissy storming through the doors.

twenty

"He claims that she's very much his *ex*-fiancé of a year ago," Sissy said while stirring her cup of Blueberry Bliss tea. Nicki shook her head and thought, "Don't start girl..." then stood and walked over to the stove. She took two apple fritters from the cookie sheet and placed them on a plate, cut them in half and returned to the kitchen table.

"Why do you doubt him," Nicki asked after setting the plate between them and taking her seat. She sipped from her tea cup then helped herself to a fritter.

"I don't know girl, call it the fear of being played by another guy. My heart just can't take it. Why do you think I purposely stay to myself?" Sissy said with frustration.

"You're getting too far ahead of yourself," Nicki reminded her. "Robert really likes you, I can tell. Don't let this ex-whatever-she-is get the best of you. Come on now, you're better than that."

Sissy paused, absentmindedly stirring her tea before answering her friend. Maybe she *was* over reacting and needed to put a little more faith in Robert.

"Well, I have to admit that he told me right away that he didn't bring her up in our previous conversations because..."

"...she's part of his past," Nicky completed the sentence.

"Yes," Sissy admitted.

"OK, then leave it at that and try to enjoy that handsome man who's obviously very fond of you."

Sissy took a bite out of her fritter and spoke between chews. "But she said she wanted to speak to him about something."

107

"Maybe she has some gold bullion she forgot to give him when they split up," Nicki said through a light chuckle. "Either way, don't you dare start up a mess over this Candice character, she's not worth it. Don't let me pull Angela in on this. You know she'll tell you a thing or two about yourself."

"Don't I know it," Sissy agreed. She let out a deep sigh then picked up the china tea cup and swallowed the last of her drink. After returning the cup to the saucer, she let out a laugh that startled Nicki."

"What?" her friend questioned her.

"I just thought about what you said. Calling Angela about this would be like putting a piece of meat out in the water for a shark. She'd gobble me up and spit me out all torn to shreds while her teeth dripped with blood."

"That's nasty Sissy, but oh so true! I think Angela is the original *Jaws*." The two women laughed at the analogy then cleared the dishes from the table.

"Well, thanks for letting me crash on your couch but I need to get home. Are you sure you're alright?" Nicki asked. She knew her friend had a way of hiding her feelings.

"I'm fine baby girl. Thanks for letting me babble."

"Any time," Nicki waved off the comment.

Sissy walked her friend to the foyer where they hugged before Nicki stepped out the door.

"Down girl," Sissy whispered her personal mantra as she made her way upstairs. Grateful for having the day off, she headed to her bedroom to start a cleaning spree.

twenty one

The mood of the upcoming season swirled around the city on the tails of biting, cold winds and falling temperatures. Along the streets of the Country Club Plaza, workers placed the finishing touches on the Christmas lights that would sparkle in all their glory from Thanksgiving Day until mid-January.

Angela's "sparkle" on the other hand had yet to return, it was still a hostage to Cody's betrayal. "I can't be a prisoner forever! He put me in this cage, but it's up to me to escape, and I know *just* the way to do it."

Winston Beck was Angela's current flavor of the month, a thirty-something software designer who usually spent the weekend chained to his computer. "I guess there are all sorts of cages in this world," she mused, "and I'm gonna be the key to unlock his!"

"Shoot, that wind is serious," Angela squealed as Winston grabbed her by the waist. It had been a little tough pulling him away from his computer for a Saturday outing on the Plaza, but Angela was determined to reestablish her mojo.

"Come here baby, I'll keep you warm." He gave her a quick hug then continued his history lesson. "Did you know that the installation of the bulbs began in early August and are due to be tested the Wednesday before Thanksgiving? They turn the lights on at two until six in the morning for people who want a sneak peek of the upcoming event."

"Well aren't you just full of information," she commented while gaping at a Tiffany & Co. window display as they rounded the corner.

"I like quirky stuff like that. Here's something else I bet you didn't know. The tradition started with a single strand of sixteen colored light bulbs over a doorway of the Suydam building in 1925, which was the Plaza's very first building. As the shopping area grew, so did the custom of hanging lights. The very first lighting celebration was in 1930…"

Angela rolled her eyes, it was fifteen minutes later and he was still rambling on.

"…and that's how the tradition that signals the start of the Christmas season in Kansas City began," he ended with pride.

"Very interesting. So, sugar, could we grab a bite to eat at the Cheesecake Factory and then take a peek in Tiffany's?"

"Sure, hon, whatever you want! Hey did you know that there's a cathedral nearby that has a Tiffany designed stained glass window? You want to check it out after lunch?"

"The lock to this cage just might require a safecracker!" Angela muttered.

Sissy pulled and shoved several storage totes from her basement to the first floor of her townhome. With the sounds of smooth jazz Christmas music playing in the background, she sat on the couch in the living room and exhaled deeply as she looked all around her, giddy with the excitement of the upcoming season and the thought of celebrating with family and friends.

"Now Robert will be able to experience firsthand all sixteen of my Christmas trees," she laughed, imagining the look on his face when he finally comes face to face with her creations.

Sissy thought for a moment. It really wasn't work for her. She truly loved Christmas and the whole meaning behind it. For her, it was a joy that poured from her heart outward when she decorated her home and invited family and friends over for tea, snacks and luncheons.

"Wow," she sighed. "It's been two years since I've had the chance to entertain at home."

In the past, her contracts always spilled over into the holiday season, preventing Sissy from returning to Kansas City.

"I'm tired of being content with just a brief 'Merry Christmas' over the phone and missing grandma's famous pineapple pancakes. This year it's going to be different…in more ways than one," Sissy said with a smile as she opened a large brown box and began pulling out the pieces to the first tree to be decorated, "…just wait until he sees it!" she giggled.

Nicki and Sammy, the company's receptionist, stepped back and admired their handiwork. The six-foot artificial tree looked like a display from one of the neighboring department stores. Toy airplanes, delivery trucks along with miniature characters and crates weaved in and out of the trees branches.

"I think we knocked it out of the ball park," Sammy said with her South Carolina drawl. She placed her hands on her hips and lifted her chin slightly with a sense of pride, being careful not to step on the pair of beige high heels that she'd taken off and replaced with ballet flats during the decorating session.

"You're so right," Nicki nodded. "I love the theme we chose, the methods used for transportation and delivery. After all we are a shipping import and export company."

"That has just acquired a huge account in Paris, France," Sammy sang out.

"High five on that," Nicki said as the two women slapped hands. "I love the red, white and blue ribbon that you used to trail down the sides of the tree."

"How about those boxes that you wrapped? That was such a clever idea using that vintage paper covered with miniature Eiffel Towers."

Nicki snapped her fingers and said, "Oh, don't forget to tell your brother thanks again for making the billboard replica with the company's logo on it. It looks so good on the top of the tree."

"Girl, he said he had so much fun making that thing. He works so hard at his job as an architect that it gave him a chance to step back into his childhood. You should have seen him putting that sign together. You would have thought he was preparing a presentation for some high paying client." Sammy giggled as she recalled the sight.

"And now, for the finale, Madame!" Sammy stepped back into her heels, walked over to the socket behind the tree and plugged in the lights, "Voilà!"

The two women cheered like school girls. "I think we deserve a recess after all this hard work, don't you, how about some lunch?" Sammy beamed.

"Yeah, I'm starving, but you go ahead, Sammy and I'll catch up with you in a minute, I have something to do." The woman nodded and departed for the cafeteria.

Nicki stood still in front of the tree. It was beautiful. She reached for one of the vintage wrapped boxes and stared at the Eiffel Tower.

"Even if I pass out from trying, I'm going to keep on exercising so I can stand right here in front of you," she whispered while touching the iconic symbol of Paris. She gently placed the box back on the tree and hurried down the hall to the cafeteria.

twenty two

"Well Mrs. Connors, if you use the wall covering in either the Fireball or Thorn color scheme I don't think you could go wrong."

Angela waited patiently for the eccentric chef and food writer to make a color decision for her home office that was going through reconstruction. Marie James had asked for her opinion as she taped each sample to the wall while stepping in front of Angela just as she was about to take a measurement.

"Just remember that the outlets for your wall lighting will be located to the left and right and close to the baseboards."

"Yes, yes, I know…I just wish that I could make up my mind on these colors," Marie said in a dismissive tone.

Angela was just about to throw the tape measure at the woman's head when Paul Michaelides, the architect crossed the threshold.

"Hey, Angela," he said loud enough to distract her. "Did you try the pastries that Marie left in the kitchen for the crew?"

"No, I didn't," she said while pretending to choke the woman behind her back.

"Well, I suggest that you do." He grabbed her hand and quickly tugged her away from Marie. When they were down the hallway out of earshot he turned Angela around to face him.

"Look kiddo, I know she's grating on your nerves and getting in the way, so why don't you knock off for the rest of the day."

"For two hours I've tried to deal with her. When I attempt to prep that room and place the measurements for you guys she distracts me with something else. I'm sorry you had to see that."

"No worries," he said. "She can be a pain at times. That's why I don't step inside this two story monster unless I have to."

Paul's crooked smile sent a zing through Angela's heart. His Mediterranean coloring brought out his large, soulful, black eyes and long lashes. She didn't exactly find him attractive, but there was definitely a sensual air about him. He wore his thick, black hair cut short with a swirl of curls that lay at the base of his neck, and his irregular nose reminded her of someone who had done a lot of street fighting. She watched as his thick eyebrows knitted with concern.

"Angela," he called her name again.

"Huh?"

"Are you alright? I've been calling your name and you just stared at me. Come on and try one of these mini chocolate cakes. Maybe your blood sugar is low."

Angela shook her head as though she were coming out of a dream. "Sure and then I'll take you up on your offer and go home."

"Yeah, that's fine." He led her down the hallway and into the kitchen giving Angela a chance to look at his six-foot frame from the back.

"Yum, yum," she whispered. His heavy-built, athletic physique caused her to move her head back and forth while she hummed the song, "Shakin" by Eddie Money.

Once inside her car, Paul came to mind again. It puzzled Angela that she would even think of him. After all she never dated outside of her race and yet her skin tingled in his presence. He had the air of a man who didn't need anyone, but for some crazy reason she could see herself in his muscular arms while her hands played with those curls at the base of his neck. Just as his lips hovered above hers she shook her head to erase the image.

"Get a hold of yourself girl," she said while rubbing her forehead and taking a deep breath and releasing it. "That will *never* happen." She placed the key in the ignition, shifted into gear and sped down the mile long driveway.

Angela stopped at Panera to pick up dinner. She didn't feel like cooking and at the last minute decided that she would stay at the restaurant and hide away in one of the booths. Fifteen minutes later she was blowing on a spoonful of potato soup as she turned the pages of *Dwell* magazine, trying to concentrate on the photos, but seeing Paul instead.

"Why do I keep thinking of him. We've only spoken on the phone a few times and our paths rarely cross because of our work schedules—the few times that we've met in the office was just to compare notes. But I have to admit, he's really intelligent and his work is impressive...and he *is* kind of stimulating..." Her phone chimed with the three bell signal that she used for Winston.

"Hey sugar," she purred.

"Hey yourself," he said. "So are you up for dinner with me this evening?"

"Sorry Winston. I had a rough day with one of my clients. The architect I work with caught me acting out my aggressions behind her back."

"Oh man," he said.

"Yeah, tell me about it. But he was cool and told me to take the rest of the day off."

"Well, I could stop by your place if you want."

"Could you give me a rain check? I'm worn out. I just want to eat my salad then slide into a bubble bath for the evening."

"Too bad I can't join you," he hinted.

"Maybe on the next one," she cooed.

"Bet," he said. "Well I'll let you get back to your dinner. I'll talk to you tomorrow."

"Thanks and goodnight." She clicked off the phone, happy to be alone again...except for Paul, who just refused to leave her thoughts.

twenty three

"Gobble, gobble," Nicki said as she slid into the passenger seat of Sissy's car.

"Good morning to you too," Sissy remarked with a slight chuckle.

"Oh my goodness, it's cold out there! I can't believe that I'm alive and ready to shop at four in the morning. And it's the day after Thanksgiving too?" She rubbed her hands in front of the heating vents before turning around to look in the back seat. "Hey where's Sleeping Beauty?"

Sissy made a left at the next corner. The block was quiet with the exception of one other car traveling down the road. Maybe another early bird shopper she thought. Finally she answered. "I called Angela twice and told her to get her behind out of bed."

Nicki pulled a slender, pink thermos from her purse. She unscrewed the top and inhaled the steam given off by the rich, hot chocolate. "Would you like to try some of my special Black Friday brew?"

"No thanks. I'll wait until I can get a cup of hot tea at Starbucks," Sissy said while pulling into Angela's driveway.

"Let me go after your highness," Nicki joked. "And she'd better be ready. I have a list with cash in hand and I can't wait to hit those early bird sales." She made a quick sprint to the front door. After three attempts at the doorbell, Angela finally answered. Her hair was pulled into a ponytail and her face was void of any make-up.

"Well, don't you look fresh," Nicki said as she stepped inside the house.

"Not now," Angela began in a gruff voice. "Hold on until I've had my first cup of coffee and then we can play."

"Whatever," Nicki answered. "In the meantime grab your coat so we can go. Sissy's waiting."

"Hold on, chick. I need my heavy duty wool one for this kind of weather." Angela walked over to the hall closet, and pulled out a long wine colored wool blend walking coat and grabbed a knit newsboy cap in matching color from the shelf above. In her stocking feet, she shuffled over to the dark brown leather riding boots sitting near the front door and pulled them on with a quick tug. Finally she swung her Fossil multi brown and leather tote over her shoulder, and paused at the door to put on her brown leather gloves.

Nicki sighed, "Angela, this isn't Fashion Week. We're going to the shopping malls. It's B-l-a-c-k F-r-i-d-a-y. At the rate you're going, it'll be Christmas Eve before we get there."

Angela held up her index finger, "Nicki, this is *not* the time." Nicki trotted back to the car. "The Queen of Hearts will be arriving shortly," she laughed.

Once Angela had settled into the backseat of the car, Sissy said, "You're working that coat and boot ensemble Missy, oh, and I have first dibs on borrowing that purse."

"You can do whatever you like as long as I can sleep while you drive to Oak Park Mall," Angela yawned.

⸺ ✦ ⸺

For three hours, the girls pushed, shoved, snatched and grabbed their way through Black Friday. In between each shopping session, they maintained their strength with liberal portions of tea, coffee, and Lamar's doughnuts. The whole process started again at the Legends Outlet Mall.

Six hours later, they called it quits as they sat down to a late lunch at Red Robin.

"Nicki, if you mention one more department store or outlet to me, I'll scream," Sissy said after downing a full eight ounce glass of water without coming up for air. "I'm so dehydrated I could drink up the Missouri River,"

"Well, that's some mighty fine drinking," Nicki teased.

"I'm starving," Angela chimed in after plopping down into their booth. When the waitress arrived, Angela turned to her and said, "Baby, just bring me the cow; hooves and all." Everyone broke out laughing, including a couple that sat at a table across the aisle from the group.

The greying, slender waitress didn't miss a beat, "I'll see if I can wrangle ole' Bessie up for ya'," while taking their orders.

"Well, I think we did well for ourselves." Nicki spoke as though they had completed a half marathon in record time.

"That might be true, but I am so ready to go back to bed!" Sissy said yawning.

"I feel you on that," Angela added. "I'm turning off my phone when I step through the door, if not before. I don't want to speak to anyone."

"Not even, what's his name?" Sissy teased as she snapped her fingers.

"Oh yeah," Nicki joined in, "what is the name of your newest flavor of the month?"

"Never mind what his name is, you two nosey women. I said no one! I don't care if it's the Wizard of Oz trying to contact me." They all cackled.

When their drinks arrived, Sissy raised her glass. "Let's drink a toast. To my girls. May this holiday season bring us much love, lots of happiness and so much joy that you won't be able to contain it."

"Amen," they all said to the sound of clinking glasses. Little did they know that their wishes would come true in due time.

twenty four

Christmas Eve finally arrived bringing peace, happiness – and for Angela a seriously bad attitude. She couldn't believe Oscar, her current fling, as she eyed the gift sitting in her hands. The "present" had been hastily swathed in crumpled gift wrap sporting a vintage Rudolph print and the crooked bow on top looked like it had seen better days as well. On cue, Angela cooed and purred, "Oh you shouldn't have," in her sexiest voice all the while her brain yelled, "You cheap, down trodden little…"

"You know you're my baby. I have one more gift for you but it won't arrive for two days. I didn't want your Christmas to be without something to open."

Angela reluctantly accepted the excuse and kissed him on the cheek before placing the gift under the tree.

"You really like the Christmas season," he smiled, admiring the five foot spruce tree decorated with snowmen and Santa Clauses made of glass, wood, and fabric; all topped off with an elaborate gold and burgundy bow with matching ribbons cascading down the sides of the tree. "Babe this is beautiful. It reminds me of my childhood and the fun I used to have with my family putting up the tree and decorating it." Oscar pulled his smart phone from his pocket and clicked a couple of pictures. Angela was moved by the gesture.

"Well, I have to get to work," he said, stuffing the phone into the back pocket of his United Airlines mechanic's uniform. He pulled her into his arms and nuzzled her neck then slid his lips across hers then nibbled on her bottom lip.

"So, will I see you on Christmas day?"

"Maybe, I'm not sure." He released her and walked to the front door. "My father's flying in from Richmond, Virginia, which is a surprise since the ole' man doesn't like to travel in the first place. I'd like to spend some time alone with him."

"Of course," she said aloud but felt a little miffed that he didn't want to stop by for a few minutes prior to seeing his father. After all, it was Christmas."

He kissed her forehead and hurried out the door. "I'll call you tomorrow," he yelled over his shoulder. "Merry Christmas!"

"Yeah, yeah," she mumbled then closed the door. When she heard the Ford F-150 pull off, she rushed over to the tree, snatched up the box, and sat on the couch ripping away the crumpled gift wrap. She had to give him credit for at least wrapping the thing and not dropping it into a handle bag with tissue paper draped on top.

She opened the white box and removed the red and green tissue inside, digging around trying to find the gift within. Her hand finally landed on something small with a slightly rough texture. She brought the plum, frosted bottle into view. She turned it around noticing the words that said, "One point one ounce." At first she assumed it was perfume but after a second look she noticed the word "musk."

"What the …" she hissed. She peered closely and noticed that the contents of the bottle stopped well below the neck.

"This better not have been someone else's stuff he's passed off on me." She pitched the bottle back into the box, grabbed her cell phone and hit the speed dial to Sissy's line.

———— ⸙ ————

"Calm down Angela, it's not the end of the world,"

"Maybe not, but it may be the end of him."

"When and if you see him again, just hint that the bottle looked a little used and go from there. Or you could say that musk doesn't suit you and give the thing back."

"I'll think about it," she fumed, "but this has put a black mark in his book."

"Poor Oscar," Sissy began, "if he keeps it up, he'll find himself on the junk pile with all your other used boy toys! But seriously Angela, ever since Cody your, love life's been like a revolving door, you never keep anyone around long enough to give them a chance."

"I know, maybe I'll get it together next month, you know, 'New Year New You.' Well I have a few things to do, I hope that *you*, at least, have a Merry Christmas."

"Merry Christ—" the click of Angela's phone rang in Sissy's ear.

Nicki pulled the sheet and blankets from her face and stared at the celling. It was Christmas morning, a cold and lonely one, or so she thought, until she spotted a daddy longlegs skitter back and forth without a care in the world near the overhead light. As a child, she used to be fascinated by bugs and would read about them constantly. She remembered her science teacher had told her that people confuse daddy longlegs with spiders. "They're similar to spiders and share some of their characteristics, but in fact they're not spiders. For one thing all spiders produce silk, but these particular creatures do not produce silk; another difference is that they have two eyes, whereas spiders usually have eight," he explained.

She was grateful that the creature stayed in the corner of her bedroom because if it had fallen on her, Nicki knew she would lose her mind. "How sad," she complained to her long-legged visitor, "it's Christmas morning and you're the only company that I have."

Oblivious to Nicki's comments, the eight-legged creature moved on to another section of the bedroom. Just as she was about to retreat back under the covers, the cordless phone rang, startled, she pushed the button, "Hello?"

"Hey Nicki, its Sissy. Merry Christmas."

"Same to you, girl. So how's your holiday so far?"

"Boring. That's why I called you."

"Thanks a lot."

"No, no, I didn't mean it like that," Sissy giggled.

"I know Sis, I'm just messin' with you. So, what's up?"

"Would you like to grab some breakfast before the crowds take over? I was thinking of going to Ms. M's. Café"

"I might as well. It'll beat watching an eight-legged creature playing on my celling."

"A what?"

"Never mind. I can go but I must report to the food kitchen at the Mission by noon."

"I'll meet you at the Café in forty-five minutes. I'm almost dressed."

"That'll work for me. By the way, are you inviting Angela?"

"Yes, if she picks up the phone. Now that she has a new boy toy, she may not have time for us."

Angela hadn't entered the old brick and stone Catholic Church in quite a while. OK, if she were being honest with herself, it was more like a few years. She sought her prayers under a different roof now.

Her mother called the night before and asked that she join the family at Our Lady and the St. Rose on Christmas morning.

"You know this is your childhood home of worship and a family tradition. Your father expects all of us to be there," her mother reminded her.

"Yes, mama," was all she dared to say.

If she declined, her father would pick up the extension to join in, leading into an all-out mini war. When he got started, Angela felt that satan himself would knuckle under to her father's pressure.

Later that morning when she walked through the faded oak doors of the building, she found her mother in her beautiful dark green, bi-corn velvet hat. It was bedecked with gossamer ribbon and a plume. As the spouse of a choir member with long ties to the church, she sat in the first row. Beside her were Angela's siblings, Frances and her brother Evan. Their spouses and children spilled over into the second row of pews.

She quickly greeted everyone, kissed her mother on the cheek and walked away as the older woman's words, "Why do you always have to be the last?" trailed behind her. Angela took her place next to her eight year-old nephew, Devon.

The choir stepped from behind the doors of the back room and took their places. The organ's rich sound signaled everyone to rise as the entrance procession began. The Mass of the Nativity of the Lord was underway. When Angela saw her father stand with the other choir members, her heart swelled as she beamed at him decked out in his gold robe with large, black scripted, first and last initials of his name, on the front.

They sang, "Hail Holy Queen," a song she remembered from, *Sister Act.* Of course, the movie version of the song was more hip, unlike the solemn version they were singing now. It didn't matter to her. She loved it because her dad belted it out. Angela's eyes drifted to the water stained walls behind the choir and the neighboring cracks that trailed below. How she remembered the stained glass windows as a glint of sun pushed through them, making the robe that Jesus wore appear like a rich Bordeaux wine!

The words of the homily seemed to drift past her ears as she stared at the fourteen small sculptures attached to the walls of the church depicting the crucifixion of Jesus. "The Stations of the Cross", the stained glass windows, the statues, all these things she had taken for granted as a child, but now…

She tugged at her coat, pulling it closer as a chill creeping across her chest made her shiver. A smile crossed her lips briefly as she looked at the old radiators that used to warm the church. As a child she remembered that her dad had volunteered his services on Sunday mornings, leaving an hour ahead of the family, so that he could start up the boiler to get the metal contraptions in working order before the parishioners arrived for the first Mass of the day.

Angela was admiring the large collection of red poinsettias that sat at the base of the white altar when she heard the priest say, "…let us offer each other the sign of peace." Bodies swarmed like bees released from a hive, as hugs and handshakes flowed throughout the church. Feeling a little ashamed that she had zoned out for half of the Mass, Angela turned around in her pew to shake hands with a neighbor when she noticed someone looking in her direction. She recognized the beautiful, dark skinned woman almost immediately.

"Candy? Candy McCall, is that you?"

"The one and only," the moon-faced, high-cheek boned woman said in a chirpy voice while embracing her friend. Candy was taken aback when she realized it was Angela. She tried to use her best poker face to conceal her shock at seeing her friend with so much extra weight.

"It's good to see you in the ole' neighborhood again."

It was too late, Angela had already detected the surprise in Candy's eyes and suddenly Sissy's words about losing weight came back to her, "Look, I'm not trying to hurt anyone's feelings, but it's time to get real."

"And I see you're still as beautiful as ever," Angela smiled.

"Aww stop." Candy swatted Angela's arm playfully and hugged her one last time before returning to her pew, but the surprise on Candy's face lingered in Angela's thoughts.

Nicki moved from one counter to the next while placing hot pans of food in the racks atop the Bunsen burners as the other volunteers prepared to serve the homeless. It was a tradition for her to assist at the missions and church kitchens during the holidays. She saw it as a way of giving back and showing gratitude for her blessings. It was sad to see so many in need of a hot meal on this day of the Lord's birth.

Several of the volunteers decorated the dining area. A six-foot tree filled with colorful ornaments and candy canes gave the room a festive look. Small gifts, a choice of gloves, socks or hats, were wrapped to give to the adults. Red stockings filled with fruit, candy and pocket-sized toys for the children were piled under the tree with a portly Santa standing at the ready. As they counted down the time before opening the doors, Nicki knew that the day would be a long one.

After eating a plateful of turkey, green beans, salad, whipped sweet potatoes, buttered corn, hot dinner rolls and Cherry Hi-C, Angela was stuffed. With all the food that stretched across three long tables, she was not ashamed to make another plate for her dinner tomorrow. She always enjoyed hanging out with relatives from the paternal side of her family. Her cousin Terrance called her name just as she sat the plates on the floor of her car.

"Hey, you want to go for a spin in my Corvette?"

"Check you out! What year is this little monster?"

"A twenty-thirteen."

"And it's in my favorite color, black. Sure why not. Let me grab my purse."

When they were on the highway, Terrance scrolled through the songs on the car's playlist, punched a few buttons and they began to jam to the music. He waited until, "Watch Out" by Lauren Hill finished while they were cruising around Wyandotte County Lake, when he lowered the volume.

"So what's up with you cuz?" he asked while speeding up to pass a slow moving, dark blue Plymouth Voyager in front of them.

"What do you mean? And by the way, remember the roads are narrow around this section. I'd like to live a little longer than just right now."

Terrance laughed and held up one hand. "My bad, sorry about that. Now tell me what happened to that cat you were dating? I didn't see him at the dinner."

"Oh that. Well, Cody forgot to tell me that he was married with children."

"You're lying! Man that is so jacked up."

"Yeah, tell me about it. But it's cool. The girls and I helped him to have a 'Come to Jesus Meeting.'"

"A what?" he asked with a puzzled look on his face.

Angela proceeded to give an abbreviated version of the Cody showdown. When she finished, her cousin let out the loudest howl of laughter she had ever heard while he pounded his fist on the steering wheel. As she thought of the scene that took place in the driveway of his house, her chuckle spilled into out and out hilarity.

"Man I wish I could have been there with my camera," he snorted. "I bet you didn't realize you could pack such a punch did you?

"I've never been that mad or hurt before," she admitted.

Terrance turned right to exit the lake area and head down the street. They'd been away for an hour and knew it was time to return to the party. He sped up on the entrance ramp and merged into the light traffic before speaking.

"Well cuz, I'm sorry that jerk treated you like that. Believe it or not, he'll get his in due time. It's a good thing I wasn't there 'cause I would have messed him up."

"No, I couldn't have you damage those skilled hands. You need them when you assist the doctors in surgery. We don't want the local news blasting you all over the air waves. I can see it now, 'Physician's assistant held for murder of punk military officer,'" she snickered.

"It's obvious that he didn't realize the jewel he possessed,"

"Aw boo." She leaned over and kissed her cousin on the cheek. "You handsome, single, dark piece of chocolate. Why, did you have to be related to me? I would have snatched you up in a heartbeat."

"Oh well, what can I say? I'm in such high demand."

"Whatever." Angela gave him a playful jab in the ribs.

"This one's for you cuz." He scrolled through the music listing until "Treasure" by Bruno Mars appeared on the screen. They started singing along as he headed east on I-70.

—⚬⚬⚬—

Now that Nicki had returned home she turned on the radio in the kitchen and adjusted the dial to the classical music station. After working at the Mission, she chose to visit with her family for the remainder of the holiday afternoon. With boxes spilling from her arms, Nicki's parents lovingly scolded her about not coming around more often. She was shocked that her father had noticed the meager amount of weight that she'd lost stating, "You're not as puffy in the face." That was as close to a compliment as she would ever get from him.

Her brothers, Maurice, who was currently engaged, and Foster, along with his wife and family of one girl and twin boys kept the energy going in her parents' home. But now she found herself alone with her thoughts on Christmas evening. She sat at the dinette and picked up the journal and pen and jotted a quick note.

It's time to relax after the madness of the day. It felt good to work at the mission. It's so sad to see so many families in need. My parents along with my brothers and their happy bunch were glad to see me. Unfortunately, my job and increased hours have kept me from them. This is a poor excuse. I must do better in that regard. Daddy noticed my weight loss which shocked me. I guess I've been so big for so long that the slightest change is noticeable.

I'm up to three days in the gym for forty-five minutes. Lately I've started to walk for one minute and alternate jogging for a minute. This I do for a total of thirty minutes. During the last fifteen minutes I just walk. The thought of accompanying my boss to Paris and Sissy's upcoming birthday trip to Savannah, helps me to stay focused on my goal.

Nicki pushed the journal to the side and stepped from the table while stifling a yawn. She made her way into the living room, settled on the couch and with the remote control in hand clicked on the Hallmark channel. A holiday movie marathon was in progress and she snuggled down to enjoy the show, but as she stared intently at the screen her heavy eyelids fluttered closed and all she could see was a slimmer Nicki standing in front of the Eiffel Tower.

—⁂—

Sissy slowly opened her eyes. They felt as though glue held them together. When she looked around the room, everything seemed off, even the pictures on the walls weren't hers and she bolted upright.

"Baby, what's wrong?" the gravelly voice below her asked.

"Oh, man. I guess I lost it for a minute. I didn't realize I was that tired." She swung her legs from the couch placing her stocking feet on the floor. After a deep stretch and yawn she attempted to stand but felt a slight jerk and landed on top of Robert.

"And where do you think you're going." He wrapped his arms around her waist and pulled her on top of him again. "I didn't say you could go yet. I don't appreciate you disturbing my sleep. You're the best blanket I've ever had."

"Oh really? Even with all my clothes on?"

"Well, you could take them off...slowly if you want," Robert said in a seductive voice. He reached up and playfully started to unbutton the top of her blouse.

"You're so sexy and too tempting." She leaned in and kissed his cheeks, then stuck out her tongue.

Robert slid his hands behind her head and opened his mouth taking her offering, slowly pulling it in and sucking on it slowly. Sissy moaned and tried to push herself away, well maybe not so much, and found that she matched his passion. She could not believe such emotion and desire resided in her. Had it really been that long since her last relationship? The warmth that overtook her body felt like a slow heat that began to burn hotter. Sissy felt greedy; wanting more of him when suddenly he broke away from her lips.

"Wow. You're so desirable Sissy. I'm so glad I met you." He rubbed her shoulders and then pushed her backward as he sat forward. "You're tempting me and I'm such a weak soul."

"Oh yeah, it's my fault." She gave his stomach a light punch then jumped off the couch and ran to the hallway.

When he caught up with her, he pushed her arms behind her back and held his lips inches from hers. "You have no idea how wonderful you are. When you do, then you'll understand how much I want you."

She stared at him as he leaned in placing a kiss on her collarbone; dragging even more kisses to the left and right before releasing her hands. He raised his eyes and said, "Thank you for spending part of your Christmas with me. Now run on home before I change my mind." Robert walked over to the bench and retrieved Sissy's coat. He held it up as she placed her arms in. After she turned to face him, he buttoned it then looked into her eyes. "Are you going home barefooted?"

Robert had her so confused that she'd forgotten to put on the leather ankle boots he'd given her as a Christmas gift. Just as she began to walk towards the living room, he returned, boots in hand. She sat on the upholstered bench and put them on. "This is beautiful," she said while dragging her hands across the tapestry fabric.

"It was my father's. He proposed to mother on it. Later, after they married, it sat at the foot of their bed."

She stood then walked to the front door while he held it opened for her. "Call me when you get home." He stroked her left ear lobe evoking a sigh from her. "Be safe baby."

"Goodnight," she whispered.

After settling into her car, she noticed his silhouette in the open door. She wanted to run into his arms and tell him to make love to her but the thought caused her to laugh and shake her head. "He'd run if he saw all these fat rolls. I'm so stupid to believe otherwise," she said aloud. She turned on the ignition then backed out of the driveway. After giving a quick tap on her horn she drove away, back to her home and away from the lie that she, Sissy Bakersfield, was sexy and desirable.

twenty five

S issy couldn't believe her cell phone was ringing at five in the morning. "Please don't let it be the staff calling me. Drama the day after Christmas is just what I don't need," she said while stepping into her work shoes.

She picked up the cellphone without looking at the caller ID and pressed the redial button.

"Sissy," a low, barely audible voice breathed.

"Who is this?"

"It's Angela."

Immediately her skin prickled. "Girl, what's wrong. You sound strange."

"Could you come over and take me to the hospital? I've been miserable all night and in such pain. Now, I feel like I can't get my breath."

"Let me call an ambulance…"

"No!" she said emphatically. "I need you to take me. I don't want to be alone."

"OK, all right. Let me call the job and explain that I have an emergency, and then I'll be right over." Sissy clicked off the phone without saying goodbye, her heart and mind racing as she went into action.

———⸙———

A petite female in a white lab coat entered the room. Her left hand brushed at the auburn hair that grazed her shoulders, and a pair of deep-set eyes revealed signs of weariness. Her slight smile seemed more an attempt to appear pleasant for the sake of the patient in front of her.

"Hello Ms. Thomas. I'm Dr. Killington, the emergency room doctor."

Angela winced from the sharp pain on her upper, right side. "Hello."

"And I'm Sissy Bakersfield, her best friend."

The doctor nodded then spoke. "Before I begin, do I have your permission to discuss your health information in front of Sissy?"

She nodded yes.

"I've looked over your vital signs and the statements you made to the nurse. Would you mind telling me when and how long your pain has been going on?"

"Around ten-thirty maybe eleven last night, I began to feel uncomfortable, like something was stuck right here." She pointed to a spot between her breasts. "All night I tossed back and forth. I couldn't sleep on my right side without the pain increasing. If I lay on my back, I felt as though I were suffocating. I took some Pepto-Bismol but it didn't work. This morning, I felt lightheaded and short of breath."

The doctor questioned her further before giving her opinion. "Well my dear, you may have an ulcer related to one of your medications or it may be gallstones."

A nurse stepped inside the cubicle. "Sherri, I need an IV started and I'll write for some pain medication before sending her over for an ultrasound." The doctor reached out and patted Angela's hand.

"I'll be back. Hang in there."

An hour later, Dr. Killington stepped back into the room. She stood at the foot of the bed while holding a sheet of paper in her hand. "Well it's confirmed that you do have gallstones."

"Oh no," Angela whispered. Sissy stood reaching over the bedrails to hold her friend's hand.

"You have two choices," she continued. "You can go home, find a surgeon and make an appointment to have them removed or, and this would be my choice, have the procedure done now since you're already here."

Angela turned to Sissy, her eyes full of fear. Immediately her friend tried to ease the situation. "It's your call but the doctor's right. You might as well stay and just get the thing over with so you can feel better."

"OK, let's just deal with the madness." Although she tried to be light about the situation, Angela's mind raced with so many questions.

"So you want to proceed?" Dr. Killington asked once more for clarification.

"Yes ma'am."

The doctor left the room as each woman dealt with her own thoughts. Finally Angela spoke. "I guess this is the slap in the face I needed. My bad eating habits have finally caught up with me."

"Let's not worry about that right now. Try to concentrate on your health and handle the other later." The door opened and the room buzzed with movement as the nurse and the transporter prepared to move her to the medical-surgical unit.

The single patient room was awash with bodies dressed in colorful scrubs. The constant movement seemed like a magic show as Angela was transferred to her hospital bed.

"Hi," a round-faced, blonde woman with bangs peered through the crowd. She stepped forward, her pear-shaped figure apparent. "My name's Coco and I'll be your nurse this evening. Unfortunately, the pre-op team will be here in a few minutes to take you to the operating room so we need to prep you right away. I hope you don't mind answering some basic questions for me while the tech works with you," she rattled on.

"No, go for it," Angela slurred.

"I'll step out so they can get you settled in," Sissy whispered.

"Oh no you don't, you keep your behind right here." Angela held Sissy's hand in a death grip until it began to throb with pain.

"OK, OK, but let me get out of their way in the meantime. Besides I need to regain some circulation in my hand," she said while shaking out her crushed digits.

Arms and hands were a flutter, clothes and underwear came off, replaced by a bland hospital gown and a pair of white, thrombotic stockings yanked roughly over her calves. A blood pressure cuff began to swell on her upper right arm as the assistant held the thermometer that poked out of Angela's mouth. Sissy stepped over to tuck her friend's long tresses under the blue paper bonnet. She gave her shoulder a quick pat before stepping out of the away again. As the clutter of bodies disappeared, Nicki peeked around the corner.

"What you won't do for attention."

"I'm happy to see you too," Angela grimaced while pulling the gown loose from her neck.

"So what's the verdict?"

"Gallstones," Sissy answered. "The beauty queen will have to endure a few days without make-up.

"How much you want to bet on that?" she said with a growl. "By the way Sis, could you go by my place and pick up a few things for me. I'll need my toothbrush, comb set, my MAC make-up..."

"Slow down your highness", Nicki interrupted. "Could you just get through the surgery first?" Before Angela could answer, there was a knock at the door.

A gentleman in brown leather shoes, stepped into the room. Six-two in height and with a dark-complexion, he stood at the foot of the bed. Dressed in coco brown slacks and a chocolate colored turtle neck, his demeanor was that of a businessman. The stranger's broad shoulders reminded one of an inverted triangle; a firm chest, small waist and no sign of fat hinted that he made strong attempts to stay in shape. Each woman, lost in their own wicked thoughts, stared at him while Angela made a low, throaty growl.

"Good afternoon, or rather, evening ladies," he corrected himself after glancing at his watch. "I'm Dr. Mark Reynolds, Ms. Thomas' surgeon," the husky voice stated.

"Mamma mia," Nicki whispered.

His luminous black eyes crinkled at the edges at the overheard comment. The close cut, black and slightly greying hair, caused his round face to stand out even more. He moved closer to the right side of Angela's bed and asked permission to speak of her impending surgery in front of her friends.

"They're more like my family," she said with a smile.

"Before this onset of pain, did you have any prior problems with eating or digestion?

"Look at me doctor? Does it look like I have problems with eating and digestion?"

He chuckled then continued with his examination. "I meant, like gas or heartburn?"

She shook her head no.

"Well, I'm sure Dr. Killington explained that you have gallstones. These are pieces of solid material that have formed in the gallbladder. There are several factors that could have triggered this. The most common are genetics, body weight, low movement of the gallbladder, diet, estrogen or diabetes." He continued his examination before going on.

"I'll more than likely do a laparoscopic cholecystectomy through the abdomen." He diagramed on Angela's body where he would make the three incisions for the procedure.

"Oh, so you're not doing the one where they pull the gallbladder up and extract it through her mouth?"

"Ewe, that's nasty," Nicki exclaimed.

With a surprised look, his eyes met Sissy's. "You've heard of that?"

"She probably has considering that she *is* a nurse or more like Little Ms. Researcher," Angela told him.

He smiled at the joke. "I think it would be best to go the laparoscopic route, with three incisions: one to the right, another in the belly button and the last below the breast bone." He retrieved a black marker from his pants pocket. "I'm placing my signature at the site so everyone will know where we're operating. Do you have any more questions Ms. Thomas?"

She nodded her head in the negative then looked to her friends and quickly asked, "What about the pain medication?"

"After surgery I'll leave orders to medicate you as needed to keep you as pain free as possible. Well ladies if there's nothing further, I'll head downstairs to get ready. I'll see you shortly Ms. Thomas, goodbye everyone." Before leaving, he gathered the papers he was holding into his left hand and shook goodbye with the right. When he exited the room a collective sigh seemed to be released.

Angela was the first to speak. "I should have asked what he uses on his face. Did you see how smooth and unblemished it was?"

"I was too busy checking out his butt when he walked out the door," Nicki sighed. "Did you see it? Oh, so firm!"

"No girl, the chest was it for me," Sissy said while staring at the empty space where he had stood.

"Listen to us." Angela laughed. "We sound like a pack of wolves descending on a kill." There was another knock on the door, this time Coco appeared with two surgical team members.

"It's time to go," she chirped while walking over to look at the bag of Normal Saline infusing through the I.V. pump near her bed. One of the two men pressed down on the locking mechanism under the bed then shifted it to the right so they could move the gurney into place. Once she was transferred over and the bed rails were put up, her friends followed the team to the elevator. They kissed her cheek, then were instructed on the location of the surgical waiting room.

twenty six

Poppies. She stared at the endless field of bright red poppies that drifted over the horizon like a raised carpet. At least in Angela's world they did. How happy she seemed to be until a voice, hazy but familiar called out her name.

"Angela, wake up. You're back in your room."

It was that chirpy-voiced person again. Why wouldn't she go away and leave her alone? To appease the woman, she tried with all her might to open her eyes and found blobs of disjointed features in front of them.

"Oh, why won't they leave me alone?" She felt her body being pushed and shoved. Then more mumbling and finally silence. She floated away, back to her world of poppies.

"Five, four, three, two, one, Happy New Year!" the emcee's voice shouted across the ballroom. Confetti and balloons dropped from the ceiling and cascaded all around as people kissed, hugged, and held up their glasses before taking a drink and dancing away the first minute of twenty-thirteen.

Robert tilted Sissy backwards, pretending to be Casanova sweeping his lady fair off her feet. She giggled then became so embarrassed that she insisted that he pull her up. He righted her, but pulled her body close to his and moved his hands swiftly from her waist to her shoulders; then with deliberate movement, placed one on each side of her cheeks.

His mouth hovered close to hers before he shifted closer and pressed his lips, gently at first, to hers. She shuddered when she felt a tip of wetness beckoning to enter. Her mouth opened slightly as his tongue found the entrance and invited itself in. She was thirsty for the passion and showed him just how much. Like a dance, practiced one time too many to perfection, she did not need to coach him. He knew his place and took it like a master; in command. The music and revelry behind them became a blur as she continued to keep pace with him.

Reluctantly, he pulled away, his breath raged as he stared into her eyes. "One day, I won't stop," he whispered in her ears. "So you better be ready."

She stared at him, knowing what he meant but too ashamed of her body to give it to him. Maybe it was time to reconsider this relationship before it went too far. Her weight issue was her's alone. She cringed at the thought of him touching her imperfect body, fat rolls, and soft skin. Of course she'd lost weight, fifteen pounds so far, but too many more to go.

She shook her head to erase the images from her mind, released a sigh and followed him to the dance floor as the DJ started playing "Don't Wanna Go Home" by Jason Derulo. People pushed their way into place capturing a spot to show off their moves. Tonight was not the time to make decisions. Instead, her hips gyrated in beat to the music.

Nicki turned up the volume on her radio while Lyfe Jennings crooned, "Never Never Land." I-70 east was light in terms of traffic, at least for the moment, until all the parties let out. She enjoyed the drive in the crisp, winter air that slipped through the car window she had cracked open.

The parties. Would she ever be a part of someone's celebration, she wondered while steering the car into the middle lane that would take her to St. Louis, Missouri. Her friends would be shocked to know that on a whim, she decided to drive to the town also known as, "The

Gateway to the West." The thought of being in her apartment on New Year's Eve was too depressing. Turner Classic Movies and Robert Osborn couldn't help her tonight. Nor did she want to be a spectator of all the live television broadcasts of the New York, Atlanta or Los Angeles celebrations.

The thought of people dressed, having a good time, looking lovingly into each other's eyes, and making plans for the future was maddening. And what was she going to do? Sit there on her sofa with her personal buffet of shrimp fried rice, pepperoni pan pizza and raspberry ice tea as her favorite movies played on, while she cried in yet another New Year?

Not this time. A deep yawn escaped her pursed lips causing her to straighten up in her car seat. She looked over at the overnight tote in the passenger seat, before returning her eyes to the road. Columbia, Missouri was only thirty minutes away and she decided to stop there for the night. At least she could get some sleep and start fresh in the morning. She prayed for two things; a hotel with a vacancy and a room surrounded by quiet.

"Please don't punish me with the sound of some couple singing the praises of their love as bed springs squeaked in the New Year. *That,*" she thought, "would be enough to make me jump out the window and bring a swift end to my 2013!"

With a pillow behind her back and a tray laden with her favorites: pizza rolls from Old Chicago restaurant, sweet and sour shrimp from Pei Wei, a bottle of Asti Spumante and a small decorative pink box filled with chocolate covered cashew patties all served on an upright bed tray, Angela felt like a queen. She even looked like one with the pink, frilly paper hat perched on top of her head.

"Oscar, you really outdid yourself. There was no need to go through so much trouble."

"You're my baby, I have to take care of you. Now, I have to admit that I was really worried about you when I brought those flowers to you in the hospital; you were so drugged out. Sissy's a sweetheart, she explained everything to me and helped to set my mind at ease." He pointed at the tray. "You better eat something before your food gets cold."

"I feel so, oh I guess, odd. The pink roses were enough but this beautiful lace bed jacket and now all this…" her voice trailed off as her hands fell to her side.

Oscar used the remote to turn on the television. "Hey babe, it's that "Dick Clark's *New Year's Rockin' Eve*" program. You want to watch that for a bit?"

"Sure, why not?" she said after swallowing her pizza roll. "I know you're not expecting me to eat all this. You better get your hips over here."

He gently climbed into her bed, fearful of jostling her too much. Although her surgery was five days post op, he was still cautious.

"Oscar, I'm not made of glass. My incisions have healed and the doctor said I can go back to work after the New Year. Come over here and keep me warm." She playfully tugged on his clothes until he leaned against her.

They dined while channel surfing between the Dick Clark program and *The Twilight Zone* marathon on the Sci-Fi channel. When they were ten minutes to the top of the New Year, Oscar poured the champagne into two fluted glasses, taking one for himself after handing Angela her's. He grabbed his paper horn while she whirled the noise maker. They counted down with their host until…"Happy New Year!" Like children, they made the worst racket and then laughed uncontrollably.

When they finally gathered themselves, Oscar gently stroked her right cheek. She turned her head to face him and for the first time noticed the small cleft in his chin. It enhanced his handsome features even more, causing Angela to let out a low growl.

"Happy New Year, my queen. I want to spend as much time as possible with you. It's been three months that we've been together and we'll continue at your pace, but don't get mad at me if I press down on the accelerator just a little."

"As long as you can pay the speeding fines, you're alright in my books." He leaned into her waiting mouth giving her an idea of what he's been dreaming of.

Sissy poured a glass of cranberry juice while she waited for the water to boil for her oatmeal. Once the rolling bubbles surfaced, she stirred in the dry oats while turning down the flames to allow the contents to simmer. She walked over to the dinette and sat after a swallow from her juice.

The bright mango colored, leather journal and orange Retro 51 rollerball pen were waiting for her on the table. She'd found them in her purse last night when she dropped her keys in after returning home. Robert was very clever. Obviously, he'd snuck them in before they started watching the *Twilight Zone* marathon last night. Sissy pulled the journal towards her, opening it to the inscription page as the new leather creaked when she pressed it back. For a guy, his handwriting wasn't bad. In fact it was legible and scripted. Sissy chuckled as she visualized Robert's elementary school teacher leaning over his shoulders, complementing the young student on his fine penmanship.

"I hope these fresh pages offer a new start, a new adventure and a door to open your heart to healing. Best always, Robert." A sound that Sissy knew all too well, caused her to jump from her chair and run over to the stove. The moist, popping sound let her know that the oatmeal was overcooking as she quickly doused it with a half a cup of water to revive it. "That's what I get for daydreaming," she said aloud while stirring the oats back to life. She added dried cranberries, slivered almonds, sugar and milk and headed back to the table. After a spoonful of the thick oats, she picked up the new pen and began her first entry.

January, 2013
Robert, clever person that he is, gave this beautiful journal to me. He says it's to open the doors of my emotions. I wonder if I'm kidding myself into believing that I'm worthy of love. I can't even get a handle on my weight so how can I conceive the thought of a relationship?

"If that weatherman says one more word about "…a possible one to two inches of light snow and temperatures in the low twenties," I'll pull out my hair," Sissy spat at the skinny and slightly balding man prancing back and forth in front of a map that showed the Midwest region.

She pulled the terry cloth robe a little tighter than needed and snuggled into the arm of the couch. With the remote control in hand, she clicked through several channels, passing the sports, weather and several reality shows.

"And I don't need this one to give me any pointers to do something crazy", she mumbled after clicking through the true crime network. She stopped at the Hallmark channel when she recognized the movie, *Love Comes Softly*, adapted from the series of books of the same name by Janette Oke. Although Sissy had seen it before, she had to admit she enjoyed it so much that she didn't mind watching it again.

After a long draw on the hot chocolate that had finally cooled, her concentration was broken by the ring tone on her cell phone. Angela's name appeared on the screen.

"Well your highness, this lowly peasant is so grateful for your call."

"Are you guys ever gonna' let that queenie stuff go?"

"Not after the way you carried on after your surgery."

"What did I do that was so wrong?"

"How soon we forget. The day after your surgery, you ordered steak for lunch and shrimp fettuccine for dinner."

"Well they offered it!"

"And the make-up?"

"Girl, now you know I couldn't let Dr. tall, dark and good-looking see me all jacked up. You know I have to always be on the ready."

"So what about Oscar, or did the anesthesia cause you to forget about him?"

"Oscar who?" she laughed.

"Oh, so you have it like that? Ms. Love em and leave em. You're a mess"

"I'm just kidding. Oscar is still in the loop."

"Oh, lucky boy."

"Anyway," Angela began in a more serious tone, "I called to check on you. Are you still planning that road trip to Savannah, Georgia?"

"I think I will," her voice slightly hesitant. "My blue funk has gotten worse. My citalopram keeps me afloat but there are those days when I…" her voice drifted off.

"What?" her friend insisted.

"Never mind."

"Oh no you don't Sissy Bakersfield. No clamming up on me now."

"It's just that some days are harder than others. When it happens, all I want to do is stay locked up in the house. No phone calls, no visits from anyone, just stay alone in my world."

"Well that's not happening so you might as well get a grip and know that Nicki and I will be around whether you want us or not."

"Yeah, I kind of figured that out after Nicki practically broke down the door when I didn't call her after four days." Sissy heard Angela snicker on the other end.

"Just remember," she began, "it's all about the love."

"I got that, and she will too when I give her the bill for the damage she put on my door."

"So," Angela said, trying to get Sissy to focus on the previous conversation. "In regards to your birthday…"

"I'm going. I traded with Janice at work so I can leave Friday morning."

"Groovy. I'll call Nicki so we can work something out on our end to join you."

Sissy was still pondering her friend's sudden use of the seventies slang term, "Groovy."

"Don't get hung up on the trivial, Sissy. Just think, your girls are going to hang out with you on your birthday, hey!"

"I have to admit, that would be nice"

"OK chick, I have two consults and one meet-up with *Le Chef* in the morning. Get some rest, love ya."

"Love ya' back." Before she could say another word, Angela hung up the phone.

"My girl," Sissy said while shaking her head then turned off the television.

twenty seven

S issy had just toweled off from her shower and hurriedly dressed. For the sake of comfort she slipped on a pair of dark blue, flair legged, jogging pants, her T-shirt with various east coast lighthouses on it and her matching dark blue hooded jacket.

The trip would take sixteen hours and some odd minutes, but Sissy knew from experience that arrival time depended on the traffic and who was driving. They all agreed to split the time behind the wheel so that they could arrive sooner rather than later while allowing each person a chance to rest.

Sissy was happy that she remembered to have her birthday vacation worked into her contract. It was a personal tradition that no matter where she was, she always took a week off to celebrate. Being so used to traveling alone, this would be the ultimate toleration test before they all flew to London and Paris in a few months to visit her brother.

"Father, give me strength," she said raising her eyes skyward, and then resumed putting the last items into her backpack. The digital clock readout said six p.m. The girls would arrive shortly so she made her way downstairs, dropped the pack near her suitcase and headed into the kitchen. She had just emptied the last bag of ice over the bottled drinks and food in the cooler when the doorbell chimed. After making a quick jog across the hallway, she opened the door.

"Hey, Sis," Nicki called out while stepping inside and giving her a hug.

"Girl, close the door, its freezing out there," Angela shouted after crossing the threshold. "Oops, did I say that? Angela feigned a look of surprise. "Hey, Sissy."

"Angela, you never cease to amaze me. Where are your suitcases?"

"We left them in the car. No point in dragging them in here and back out again," Nicki informed her. "Well, what do you need us to do so that we can get this show on the road?"

"Help me take the cooler and my suitcase to the van, and then I'll come back and lock up the house."

"Van!" both women exclaimed.

Sissy chuckled. "Calm down. I'm not putting you guys in a *mommy mobile*. The technical name for it is a crossover utility vehicle aka a Ford FLEX. It has more space than my car because it can seat up to seven people. We won't have to be bunched up while traveling. The seats fold down to handle the luggage and cooler. I rented it for the trip. Come on." She grabbed her coat off the staircase railing while the girls followed her out the door after picking up the ice chest.

Once the luggage was loaded and the house was secured, Sissy agreed to take the first leg of the trip to St. Louis. Angela, who didn't mind driving in the wee hours of the morning volunteered to take over afterward. Blankets, pillows, iPads and books with night lights attached were out and ready for action.

Before Sissy started the engine, the girls paused to say a prayer for safety during their trek. She jotted some quick notations about the starting mileage and time in a pocket-sized notebook then placed various maps in the driver side door pocket.

"You have the GPS, why do you need those maps," Angela asked.

"It's a backup. These systems have a tendency to go out if you stay in an area where the signal is blocked for too long, like a forest or a long boulevard with lots of trees." She turned on her favorite station, Radio Classics, then pulled onto the street.

No matter how many times she traveled through St. Louis, Sissy always loved watching the top of the Gateway Arch come into view. Seeing the 630-foot stainless steel monument at night made it seem surreal. Memories flooded her mind as she recalled her parents driving to St.

Louis with her and William in the backseat. It was the first of many vacations the family would take. Her father, a true history buff, would spout off bits of Americana to them as they traveled the highways to their destination. He was like a kid himself, becoming as excited as they when approaching each town.

The first time she saw the gleaming landmark from a distance, it reminded her of a monster rising from the Mississippi. Yet when they finally stepped out of the car and walked up to it, she feared it would topple over.

Her father laughed, not to shame her, but at the imagination that only a child would have, while reassuring her that no harm would come to them. It was spectacular indeed and even more so when they rode to the top of the Arch and looked down at the people below. As she watched the figures mill around the base of the monument, they reminded her of the miniature doll house family in her bedroom. She was pulled from her reverie when she heard Angela's low voice saying, "Hey Sissy, Are you ready for me to take over?"

"Sure. Let me pull into this Quick Trip gas station so we can do everything at one time." She drove up to the pump and stepped out, feeling every bit of soreness in her legs and calves. Nicki sat up in the back seat, stretched then looked around and finally stepped out of the car. After filling the gas tank and personal needs were met, Angela slipped behind the wheel and made the necessary adjustments while Nicki moved up to the passenger seat and Sissy lay down in the back. It was time for her to hang out with Mr. Sandman.

Sissy awakened in a fit and bolted upright. Too many questions engulfed her mind. How long had she been asleep? Where were they and why had the car stopped? As she looked around, a tall, bulging pair of legs dressed in blue caught her attention. She scooted closer to the window and looked up to find a pair of red underpants, more blue and a large "S" emblazed on a monstrous chest. After closing her eyes, she quickly opened them again to look into those of what seemed to be Superman.

Peals of laughter and then muffled conversation from outside caught her attention. She opened the passenger door and stared at Angela and Nicki taking pictures of the fifteen foot statue. Just as she was about to ask them what in the world possessed them to do something so reckless so late at night, she watched Angela grab the calf of the Man of Steel and lean backward while running her fingers through her hair. Nicki snapped away on the camera while Angela pretended to be a high power fashion model.

"What are you two doing out here? Get in the car you, you…"

"We've been busted," Nicki called out.

"I love Superman," Angela said while running back to the car.

"Where are we anyway?" Sissy asked after sliding back into her seat and pulling the blanket over her.

"Metropolis, Illinois. I had to see it since we were in the neighborhood," Angela said sheepishly, as she started the car's engine. After a few twists and turns, she made her way back to the interstate.

"Let's use a little more caution and no more stops unless it's for the bathroom or gas."

"Yes mommy," the women said sarcastically.

Sissy shook her head while settling under the blanket allowing the motion of the car to lull her back to sleep. Angela cranked up the radio as they traveled down I-24E to exit 44 in the direction of Paducah, Kentucky.

———— ∞∞∞ ————

"Last call for the bathroom because I can't wait," Nicki said through loud stifled yawns while pulling into the busy rest area.

"Where are we now?" Angela asked before stepping from the car.

"I lost track when we switched up in Nashville. After a while, these towns all look the same." She looked at the clock on the car's dashboard. "It's five-thirty in the morning and we're outside of Atlanta. You better shake a leg and hit the can before their crazy rush hour traffic starts."

"Do you have to be so crude?"

"No worse than you," Nicki snapped back.

"Ladies, ladies," Sissy called out in a gravelly voice as she sat upright. "Let's try to be nice to one another. And by the way, good morning." The two women returned the greeting without enthusiasm while digging through their purses and overnight bags.

Sissy opened her passenger door and let out a yelp. "Oh yuck, what *is* that smell? Cow manure?"

"Yes ma'am," Angela snickered as she placed a pink and black bandana over her nose and ran into the building. The scent made Sissy cringe as she hurriedly joined her friends.

Once they had completed their morning rituals in an abbreviated fashion and returned to the vehicle, Sissy moved behind the steering wheel to take over the last leg of the journey. As her friends were getting settled, she glimpsed in her peripheral vision the yellow-orange sphere of the sun making its morning debut. She turned to face this blazing sign of life, admiring the way it rimmed the clouds above. Inwardly she said a prayer of thanks for keeping them all safe then started the ignition.

"Onward James," Angela pointed while Sissy backed out of the parking spot, switched gears then moved forward to merge into traffic.

"Look, this isn't *Driving Miss Daisy*," she replied while looking into the rearview mirror at Angela triggering bursts of laughter all around.

"Finally," Nicki sighed as they pulled up to the hotel.

"Thank You Lord!" Sissy said while parking the car and turning off the ignition. She made some notes about the journey in her book then stepped out and stretched. She looked at her watch. "It's nine in the morning. I'll ask if we can check in early while you two start pulling things together."

Thirty minutes later she returned with room keys and maps clutched in her hand. They unloaded their suitcases and other belongings, walked inside and took the elevator to the fourth floor.

The urban-styled room was designed with clean lines, a monochromatic color scheme and modular furniture. It held two full size platform beds and a full size couch that let out into a sofa sleeper. A sleek black desk, chair, dresser and plasma television completed the front of the room. Near the window, a black, contemporary recliner and floor lamp made the room more inviting. Angela pushed back the curtains to look out on the town. Once they checked the cleanliness of the room and were assured that no bedbugs resided in the mattresses, everyone began settling in.

"I'm going to take a shower then head out to St. Simons Island. I'm still wound up from the drive," Sissy said.

"I think I'll just stick around here and relax."

"Could I hang out with you on the island?" Nicki asked.

"I'd love the company! I'll hurry."

twenty eight

A long the Georgia coastline, midway between Savannah, Georgia and Jacksonville, Florida, is a treasure called the Golden Isles. Starting with the mainland port city of Brunswick, the four barrier islands of St. Simons, Little St. Simons, a privately owned ten thousand acre resort, Sea Island and finally Jekyll Island complete the Golden Isles.

Four hundred years ago, Spanish explorers seeking gold wandered upon the islands, and admiring their beauty and temperate climate, gave them the name, the Golden Isles. St. Simon's Island, with its white sand beaches and live oaks covered with Spanish moss hanging from gnarled branches, is the largest of the islands.

"Oh my," Nicki exclaimed. "Look at all that green lush area out there."

"Those are called marshlands. There's a whole ecosystem that exists out there that does more than give the land beauty. The small islands further out are called hammocks."

"I didn't realize you were into all of this," Nicki said after clicking a few pictures before Sissy started driving again.

"I had a work contract in Augusta and Savannah about six years ago. I loved traveling down this way to get a whiff of the ocean when I had weekends off. It's fun to learn about new places, so I always read up or take field trips to the areas I'm most interested in. I guess that's the geeky side of me."

"What a pretty town! I feel like I'm breathing fresh air."

"You are. The ocean is just over there." Sissy pulled into the first available space she could find and parked. "Come on. I'll show one of my favorite lighthouses."

As they walked past boutiques, shops, galleries and restaurants, Nicki became increasingly self-conscientious as she caught a glimpse of her reflection in the windows. She was grateful when they turned the corner and walked up the path through the white fence to the red-brick, Victorian designed dwelling.

Nicki snapped away at the building and the white tower that stood behind it. They decided to take a tour of the lighthouse, although Sissy had done so during her first visit to the island years ago.

"My name is James," the lanky man announced as he stepped forward. His white hair stuck out from the back of a denim ball cap with the logo of the lighthouse in the center. He was from an era when men still tucked in their shirts, wore belts to hold up their pants and laced up their shoes. His stark black eyebrows were a strong contrast to the white hair and caused his small, blue eyes to stand out even more. Nicki looked at James' features and guessed that at one time he had been a rather handsome, and possibly, charming man.

"I will be your guide today and I want to thank you for visiting St. Simon's Lighthouse. As a retired sea dog, I volunteer three days a week here. It keeps me from becoming a complete landlubber!" A couple of women behind Sissy and Nicki chuckled at the comment.

"After the tour, if you'd like, the lighthouse is open for those who want to take a crack at climbing the one hundred and twenty-nine spiral steps to the top."

He escorted them into the next room filled with pictures and equipment. "James Gould of Massachusetts built the first lighthouse here in 1810 and served as the first lighthouse keeper for twenty-seven years. It was destroyed in 1862 by Confederate soldiers to prevent Federal Troops from using its beacon. This two story dwelling and 104-foot tower was built in 1872."

As James continued with his presentation, Nicki thought of the climb to the top of the tower. She didn't want to embarrass herself, not only in front of her friend but also in front of the strangers that stood behind her. She had missed a few days at the gym and found it difficult to go through its doors again. Walking for forty-five minutes in her neighborhood or at the school track was better than nothing at all, but she knew that she pushed herself harder when she worked out on the equipment in the gym, and felt better after doing so.

"...This is one of five surviving light towers in Georgia. It serves as a navigational aid, and the light can be seen twenty-three miles out to sea," she heard him say. She purposely allowed another couple to move ahead of her when they walked over to the lighthouse.

"So who's ready to take that climb with me to the top? You will be able to see Jekyll Island, Brunswick, also known as the mainland, and the south end of St. Simon's Island." Nicki couldn't believe thirty minutes had passed so quickly. She moved to the back of the room and almost slipped out when Sissy called her name.

"What's wrong? Don't you want to see what's it's like up there?"

"No, that's OK. I'll wait for you outside."

"Nicki..."

"Go ahead, I'll be fine. In fact, I'll meet you at the beach. I want to shoot some pictures from that angle."

With reluctance, Sissy went ahead and caught up with the group that was already climbing the stairs as their guide's voice faded around the landing. Nicki walked over to the gift shop and purchased a post-card and a miniature version of the lighthouse before heading down to the water's edge.

———⊱⊰———

"So, what was that all about?" Sissy asked when she caught up with her friend near a boulder a short distance from the lighthouse.

"I just changed my mind. What's so wrong with that?"

"Nothing if that's all it truly was. I think there's something you're not telling me."

"I'm just fooling myself into believing that I can lose weight. When we were walking over here, I saw my reflection in the windows of those shops we passed by. I still look like a big ole' cow." She paused then threw a rock at a wave that lapped up on the shore.

"Stop it," Sissy hissed. "I refuse to stand here and listen to you degrade yourself."

"You don't have to. I can do a good job of it with or without your company."

"Damn."

"Sissy, I'm sorry. I didn't mean... I don't know why I feel this way."

"I'm going to walk away and do some shopping." Sissy swiped at a tear that splashed across her cheek. "You can stick around here for a while and shoot some more pictures, or better yet why don't you just drown in your own pity."

Nicki made an attempt to speak but Sissy placed her hand in the air like a school cross walk guard.

"I'll meet you back at the car around one." Nicki nodded her head in agreement and watched as her friend stormed off, putting as much distance between them as possible. When her frame disappeared around the bend past the lighthouse dwelling, Nicki gathered her things and walked further down the shore in the opposite direction.

———— ◯◯◯◯ ————

Nicki sipped on a glass of lemon infused iced tea while she waited for her meal. A middle-aged couple with two children walked in and was seated in a booth at the front of the restaurant. For some reason that she could not explain, Nicki continued to watch as the group settled into the seating area. The husband appeared older with grizzled curly hair in a misshapen afro. He wore a black T-shirt and checked print cream colored Bermuda shorts. His hairy black legs ended with white ankle socks and black tennis shoes.

When she looked at the mother, it triggered a slight distress as she wondered, "Do I look like that?" The bulky framed woman appeared disproportioned due to her weight. Rolls of flesh spilled from beneath her black tank top while her jeans revealed a sagging lower abdomen and an apron of flesh that caused Nicki to flinch. She raised her arms to release a blanket from the one year old that her husband held near him. As she caught snatches of their conversation, she briefly felt a pang of jealousy.

"It seems so unfair," she thought, "that despite her weight, clearly two-hundred pounds plus and her plain looks, that she could be happily married with a husband and two children." A waitress disrupted her musings as she placed a half chicken salad sandwich on rye bread, a cup of tomato soup and potato chips in front of her. Nicki took a last look at the family then turned her gaze to the picture window and aimlessly watched people stroll along the sidewalk.

"Go Sissy, it's your birthday, it's your birthday, let's party..." Angela and Nicki sang out while bouncing on her bed.

"Have you two lost your minds? You better stop before this thing crashes to the floor," she said as she jiggled back and forth between her friends.

"It's time to wake up," Angela shouted. "We have to celebrate your special day. So get up, brush those funky teeth, and get dressed so we can have breakfast."

"Excuse you," Sissy laughed. "Move outta my way so I can get to the bathroom." She swatted at Angela who ducked just in time.

As soon as the bathroom door closed, Angela walked over to Nicki as she untwisted the last strand of her hair.

"Did you clear things up with her?"

"Yes, before we went to bed last night. I felt bad about the way I spoke to her. I was just having one of my blue funk moments. Maybe it was just a small case of jealousy that came over me."

"Jealousy?"

"Yeah, because of her weight loss. She's doing so well and I'm at a standstill. It wasn't until we were about to climb the stairs of the lighthouse that reality hit me."

"What reality? I don't understand what you're talking about. You've lost twenty pounds, that's a great start in my opinion."

"It was, but now it seems like my fat won't move forward, like it's stuck in one gear."

Angela sat next to Nicki. "Your problem is that you're at a plateau. Your body lost so much weight in the beginning, so fast, that now it's stuck on stupid."

"Thanks a lot."

"Stop being so sensitive," she said while giving Nicki a playful shove. "It happens to everyone when they diet or exercise. That's when you have to shake it up, change things around to wake your body up to something new. When you go to the gym, try a different machine, like the rower or the stair climber. In your diet take away something you eat or drink all the time, like those colas that aren't good for you and drink more water."

Nicki gawked at Angela. "And when did you become so knowledgeable about diet and exercise?"

"I've been reading a lot of books about nutrition lately. It happened after my surgery. That was my wakeup call, my body tried to tell me that I was harming it. I wouldn't listen, so it decided to fight back. Anyway, I'm glad you two have cleared the air. I want all of us to have fun without any underlying tension."

Before Nicki could respond, the bathroom door swung open and Sissy danced into the room. She wore a pair of dark plum slacks, and a blush pink, long sleeved sweater set. She'd pulled her hair into a French twist with a whisper of bangs in the front. On top of her head sat a hat that looked like a pink frosted cake, candles scattered about with the words, 'Happy Birthday' emblazed across it.

"Well, check out the birthday girl!" Nicki squealed. "She's a hot mama today."

"I *know* you are not wearing that thing on your head?" Angela frowned.

"Oh yes I am, with pride." She walked over and sat in a nearby chair and laced up her brown leather walking boots. "What are you guys waiting for? It's time to start my special day." She grabbed her handbag and headed for the door. As they stepped outside, the cool forty-five degree air snuck in like an unwanted guest causing the girls to squeal.

The trio made their way to the Factors Walk which provided the perfect venue for the day's outing. "These old buildings on the northern end of the Historic district of downtown Savannah at one time were commercial houses. They resided below the bluff and opened in 1744," Sissy read aloud from her tour book. She guided them down a set of stairs and levels between stores and business. "The warehouses were a series of buildings interconnected by these walkways and iron bridges. These levels are where the men called *factors*, decided, or factored, the cost at which cotton would be sold."

They continued on to the steep cobblestone streets and sidewalks crowded with gift shops, restaurants, bars and antique stores on one side, and a view of the Savannah River on the other. After breakfast, they took to shopping the area, passing several strangers who wished Sissy a happy birthday as they caught sight of her colorful hat.

"I can't believe she actually did that mess," Angela remarked.

"Did what?"

"That," as she pointed at the top of Sissy's head.

Just as the party girl was about to make an unpleasant comment, a group of tourists that hovered on the sidewalk in front of them began singing the "Happy Birthday" song. Sissy gave a graceful curtsy to the group with heartfelt thanks. As they stepped past them, she turned to Angela, briefly stuck out her tongue and said, "Don't hate, let's just celebrate."

Nicki busted out in laughter, held up her hand and gave the birthday girl a high five, then turned the brass knob on a door and crossed the threshold of The Peanut Shop. Sissy paused for a moment as her eyes adjusted to the dimness of the store after having walked through the sun-splashed streets outside.

The store was just as she had remembered it. The brown and red unpainted bricks gave the building the feel of an old warehouse. Her eyes moved across the room like a lover that had found his way home. Thick brown tables and shelves held rows and rows of canned peanuts in different varieties. She turned her head in time to notice a male sales clerk with dark blonde curly hair. He looked to be in his late twenties with a pale complexion and angular build, appearing more youthful than manly. His smile, bright and inviting matched his languid voice causing her to stroll in his direction.

"Hello ladies."

"Hey," they said in unison.

"Oh, and someone's celebrating a birthday, happy special day!"

"Thank you Matt," Sissy responded after reading his name tag. "I see you have my favorite peanuts," she added, as she reached inside a grey wooden tub for the burlap bag of salted in the shell nuts.

"Feel free to sample the different flavors we have on display and let me know if you have any questions," he said before walking away.

"I'd love to sample you," she said under her breath.

Angela's head snapped as she stared at the birthday girl. "What did you say with your nasty self?"

"Huh?"

"I'm not crazy Sissy...Ooh girl, you've got to try these," Angela mumbled between bites of Hot Southern flavored peanuts.

"Wrong answer, the New Orleans Creole style is it," Nicki called over her shoulder.

They meandered throughout the store for twenty minutes, walking between store set-ups and long wooden tables full of apothecary styled oversized jars of different flavored candies. A couple of the managers moved boxes from the aisles as new displays were being arranged. Each of the women found their way to a favorite peanut flavor finally settling on one to take home.

Occasionally Sissy flirted with the clerk, giving way to her free spirit, excusing it as her birthday wish to do whatever she wanted. Just as she reached for her package, Matt placed a tiny pink pig, called a "lucky pig", in her hand as a birthday token for her day. She thanked him as they waved goodbye and stepped out the door.

The afternoon belonged to Sissy as she guided her friends along Savannah's famous squares introducing them to several mansions, including the Asendorf House also known as the Gingerbread House because of its "steamboat Gothic gingerbread carpentry," and in particular, The Mercer House, scene of the murder depicted in the famous novel *Midnight in the Garden of Good and Evil.*

"Oh yeah, I remember reading the book!" Angela exclaimed excitedly as the girls approached the notorious mansion.

"Three or four deaths happened there, right?" Nicki asked.

"Girl yeah, it was nasty. The first death was in the early 1900s when one of the owners fell over the second floor bannister and died a few days later. The next was in the in the 1960s when a kid running on top of the roof fell and was impaled on the iron fence surrounding the house."

"Oh, poor boy!" Sissy commented sadly.

"Oh, and the third one was that famous shooting, right?" Nicki asked.

"Yeah, the one that took place in the novel. This famous antiques dealer was arrested for shooting his assistant. He was tried four times for the murder – the only person in Georgia to be tried four times for the same crime. On the fourth trial he was found not guilty; he died just a few months after he was acquitted. They say it was in the same area of the house where the assistant was found murdered," Angela ended.

The girls spent forty-five minutes touring the Civil War era mansion, viewing the extensive collection of 18th and 19th century furniture, antiques, portraits and drawings. After the visit, the trio entered the gift shop.

"Oh, look! The 'Bird Girl' statue!" Sissy pointed at the little replica near the register.

"Yeah, that's the statue that was on the cover of that novel. It's at some cemetery, what's it called?" Nicki asked.

Overhearing Nicki's comment, the elderly clerk at the cash register, looked over her glasses and said, "Oh, honey, it's not at the Bonaventure Cemetery anymore. They moved that thing over to the Jepson Center on York Street."

"York Street? Do you know the full address by chance?"

"207 West York Street, honey. People ask about that all the time," she laughed.

Nicki picked up her purchase and thanked the clerk then the group headed to the museum.

After visiting "Little Wendy", the nickname the original owners had given to the iconic statue, they rounded out their afternoon dashing in and out of several boutiques and quaint shops, strolling down side streets, and visiting popular tourist haunts. Five hours later, the coolness of the air and the setting sun signaled that it was time to turn back. The day had been a long one, full of exercise not only for the body but also for the senses.

Back at the hotel, Sissy struggled to open the door with the key card, while Angela and Nicki twitched impatiently, both needing to relieve themselves.

"Girl, come on, I've got to pee!" Angela growled.

"Oh, I hate these things," Sissy complained.

Finally the door popped open, Angela and Nicki pushed Sissy roughly aside as each fought to be the first to the bathroom."

"Dang, you're welcome," Sissy said as she fell against the door.

Sissy flipped on the lights, tossed her purse on the sofa, and then she saw it: a beautiful vase full of a dozen white roses resting on the coffee table in front of the sofa.

"Oh, how pretty!"

She read the attached card: "To my Cherokee Rose – that's the state flower of Georgia. Can't wait til your sweet petals touch my lips again! Happy Birthday, Robert."

Angela emerged from the bathroom, drying her hands with a towel, "Ain't that nice, flowers."

"Well, I know who won that race," Sissy chuckled.

"But those flowers are nuthin' compared to the surprise we have for you."

"What's that?" Sissy asked excitedly.

"Can't say, just be dressed and ready for dinner by seven," Angela hinted.

———— ✸✸✸ ————

When the group paused outside The Olde Pink House, Sissy was speechless.

"Happy Birthday!" the two women shouted. Nicki flashed away on her camera as Angela ushered Sissy through the door.

A hostess led the threesome to their table, cautioning them to be careful as they climbed the narrow stairway to the next landing while the faint strains of *Spring* from Vivaldi's *The Four Seasons* played in the background.

The women took their seats at a reserved table near a window in one of the mansion's beautifully restored dining areas. As they scanned the room, they appreciated how the stately home's interior perfectly complemented its exterior.

After wine and appetizers were delivered to the table, Nicki explained why they chose the Olde Pink House as the site her surprise.

"Since you like history and wonderful old buildings," Nicki began, "we thought this would be the perfect spot for your birthday dinner. This is the former home of James Habersham, built in 1789. The Habershams were early cotton factors, and one of the founding families of Savannah. Here's how the mansion got its nickname. The building was originally covered with white stucco, but the red brick façade underneath kept bleeding through, causing the structure to take on a pink hue, and giving it the name 'the Pink House.' Eventually, in the 1920s, tired of constantly having to repaint the old stucco white, the owners simply replaced it with pink stucco."

"This mansion has quite a history," Angela continued, "it's one of the few buildings to have survived the devastating fire of 1796 which destroyed half of the city, later it served as the home of The Planter's Bank, and during the Civil War was the headquarters of Union General Zebulon York."

Sissy shook her head to stop the tears that threatened to spill forward at the thought of all of the trouble that her friends had gone through to arrange this lovely surprise for her. She held up her glass of sweet smelling, apple accented Riesling to toast her sister-friends.

"Thank you for sharing this special day with me. I know I haven't been the best person the last few weeks, and I appreciate you both for tolerating me during those times."

"Though thick and thin," Nicki began.

"Like the Three Musketeers," Angela added.

"All for one and one for all, united we stand divided we fall," Sissy quoted as they raised their glasses and clinked them over the din in the space they shared with the other diners.

Forty minutes later a waiter returned with an assistant. They placed a platter of fettuccine with sautéed shrimp and scallops covered with butter and parmesan white cream sauce in the center of the table. Another platter held asparagus adorned with slivered almonds. A basket of brown and white yeast rolls rounded out the dinner.

Laughter followed when Sissy, tempted by the rich aroma rising from the table, immediately served herself, picked up her fork, and began eating before her friends could even put food on their plates. Intense conversation ensued as they shared their meal and strengthened the bond of friendship that had held them together since childhood.

Dessert arrived festively: a triple layered white cake covered with pink frosting and adorned with an arrangement of yellow and orange candied flower petals. A trio of lit sparklers danced in the center of the cake, causing nearby diners to turn and applaud.

As the waiter placed thick slices of the luscious dessert on each plate, Angela and Nicki pulled small boxes from their purses and set them in front of Sissy. One was wrapped in coral and the other in yellow-orange, each was decorated with plenty of ribbons and concealed wonderful birthday surprises.

When a bottle of champagne arrived, Sissy laughed, "This party is definitely going to last well into the night!"

twenty nine

Hello Journal-
I can't believe that January is almost over. It seems we just ushered
in the New Year and now, in a few days we will be in a new month.
Hanging out with Sissy and Angela for the birthday bash in Savannah
was great. I have to admit that I'm ashamed of myself for the pity
party I was going through. I guess I got so hung up on 'the weight'
and what the scale revealed every time I stepped on it that I was just
making myself crazy.

Before work tomorrow, I plan to step back through the doors of the
gym and get my act together. It will only be thirty minutes but it's better
than nothing. Besides, walking outside in the cold weather is not my
thing. Truth be told, I like exercising early in the morning because I don't
have to step behind the curtain in the private booth to change clothes
when all the shapely smaller women are in the dressing room. My body
is such a disgrace, but I did it to myself. It's no wonder a man won't look
at me, all these rolls of fat. It sickens me.

Funny how Angela overlooked the point that when you're obese,
losing twenty pounds is like losing five: no one can tell the difference.
Well, I have to call it a night. Tomorrow's my first day at work after
my mini vacation. Countdown to Paris begins in the morning. After I
emptied my suitcase this evening from the Savannah trip, I placed a
few things for the overseas journey in their place to get my packing
started. Oh shoot, I just remembered, I better check the expiration
date on my passport! Here's the first French phrase that I've learned:
"Bonne nuit" which means goodnight.

———∞∞∞———

I'm so thankful that I don't have to report to work until Wednesday. I felt sorry for Angela and Nicki, they only had one day to rest after our whirlwind drive back to Kansas. They were good sports about everything and that's why I drove the last, and longest, leg of the trip back so they could rest. I love them both and adore my birthday gifts. The sterling silver, antique fork-shaped bracelet is fantastic. The way the artist bent the tines into curls and swirls is amazing. The matching earrings were perfect! How clever of the sculptor to take the bowl of the fork with the tines and design them in the same fashion as the bracelet. No one at the job will have anything like it, which makes them even more special.

My girl Nicki looked so good in her seventies throwback pant suit. The black flair leg slacks and hip waist jacket gave her a sleek look. And that white blouse with the extended wide cuffs made her look like a model out of catalog for large size women. Her twist out hairdo really accents her face. I wish she could see how beautiful she really is to others. And what can I say about Ms. Thang? She looked fantastic as usual!

I was shocked when I received my bouquet of roses from Robert. He's so thoughtful and caring. He called on my birthday during dinner, and once again before we left Savannah for the drive home. Robert's trying his best to get close or shall I say closer, but I have to watch my heart. It's been five years since the last time I let anyone get that close to me. Once I found out the truth about Franklin (the man who claimed to have an undying love for me) and what he was doing behind my back, I shut down my heart. It still hurts that he and my roommate from college were "doing the do"— and in my bed! That's a pain I don't want to experience again.

Well I better close this out and get some sleep. I have to return to my routine at the gym in the morning, after all, London and Paris are on the horizon and I have to be ready to wow the men. Ha, ha, who am I kidding?

I've been practicing a little bit of the language, let's see oh yeah, "Au revoir", I think that's goodbye. Must practice...

This is so weird-writing your thoughts on some blank piece of paper. I bet Oprah had something to do with this mess. If I'm not mistaken, I think it's some new age thing. What am I to say? Sissy says writing out what I eat will help me to keep track and control my weight. Will it control my emotions? My heart? What about the feelings of wanting to find the right man to love you and call you his baby? OK-this is a mess. I'll have to try this another time. Later!

thirty

As Sissy completed her errands, she decided at the spur of the moment to surprise Robert at his work site. The long drive home last night put her back into the city sometime after midnight. Knowing that he had to work in the morning, she didn't want to wake him once she had returned home. She neared the parking lot only to find it crowded and with limited space. Sissy made a left hand turn to exit the lot and found the unseen spot between two trucks. Her car seemed tiny next to them as she parked and carefully opened her door to squeeze out. "I'd better add a liquid diet to my weight loss plan" she joked to herself.

After three hard knocks on the metal trailer door, a gruff voiced yelled out, "Come in already."

"Well that's a fine welcome to a former birthday girl," she joked while stepping inside. He jumped up from behind his desk and in a matter of two steps, picked her up and swung her around as she squealed with joy.

"Baby! I've missed you! When did you get in? Why didn't you call me?" he asked excitedly, scarcely giving her an opportunity to open her mouth.

"Well if you'd put me down, maybe I could answer your questions." He did as she asked, taking her by the hand and offering her a nearby chair while he sat on top of his desk. She looked at him and could not believe how handsome he was. His brown eyes bore right into her and she felt a warmth creep over her like before. She compared it to hot fudge being drizzled over ice cream, creating crevices in its path as hot and cold mixed at the base of the bowl and...

"Earth to Sissy. Houston we have a problem," Robert's voice suddenly jolted her from her fantasy.

She laughed briefly, "Sorry about that, I was just thinking about something."

He stood up and reached for her hand. "Do you have time to join me for lunch?

"Yes, but I have a special request."

"If I can answer it," he said cautiously.

"You said next time that you would give me a tour of your worksite. Would today be alright?"

"Sure, I don't see why I couldn't. The guys should be on their lunch break, so the equipment is down for the moment. But first, let me see your feet."

"My feet? I didn't know you were freaky like that," she giggled.

"You wish," he teased. "I need to make sure you aren't wearing some cutesy girl shoes. We wear steel toed boots out here." She stuck out her feet so he could see her mock hiking boots.

"Next, you must wear this hard hat, that's the rule. I don't care about your hair getting messed up. Head safety is no joke." He picked up the white plastic helmet that reminded her of an oversized baseball cap and handed it to her. Robert walked over to the grey metal file cabinet and picked up his full brimmed, orange hard hat and placing it on his head.

"Stay near me at all times and be careful where you step." He opened the trailer door allowing Sissy to exit first then stopped to lock it before they went into the construction area.

He opened the galvanized steel gate and stepped in while she followed behind. Gravel crunched under her boots causing her footing to shift while she walked along the uneven surface. She noticed orange cones and yellow safety tape that cordoned off newly dug areas. The space that they entered felt cavernous as they moved downward to the first level of the building.

They passed by deep dugouts, some with wood frames inserted within. Robert pointed to an opening. "This is the first level of the parking garage. Remember the pillars I showed you the first night I brought you here?"

"That's them?" she pointed.

"Like a puzzle, see how it all fits together? Combined with the next floor it makes a stacked parking garage. After this we'll start the construction of the actual building." He took her hand as they made their way to the left of the structure and climbed up a short flight of stairs. They stepped onto the first floor of the building, and walked to the center of it.

"The Wells Fargo bank and the food courts will be over here," he said while pointing to the skeletal frames to his right.

"Your team is really making progress. I can't believe this is the same area you showed me a few months ago."

"It'll be six to nine months before it's complete as long as the bad weather doesn't delay us for too long. Hey my stomach's growling, a sign that it needs to be fed."

"Well the last thing I want is for my baby to starve so we better go," she teased.

They turned to make their way back to the trailer. Machines roared, coming to life as the men returned from their lunch break. Once inside his office, she handed the hard hat back to him.

"You know," he began as he put his gear away. "There's a sense of gratification when the job is finished but an overwhelming sadness at the same time. You leave a little bit of yourself in each project when it's completed." He cleared his throat, aware of his own sentimentality.

"Well, let's get some lunch." He reached for her hand and they headed for the door.

<hr/>

"Finally," the newscaster exclaimed, "the first day of spring will arrive at six-thirty Wednesday morning! Eventually we'll start to see a warming trend."

"Thank the Lord," Nicki answered back to the television. "I'm tired of wearing coats, boots, and all the other stuff that comes with winter." She pulled on her wool coat just as the doorbell rang. After looking through the peephole, she opened the door for Sissy.

"Hey girl," she said while steeping inside. "Spring can't get here fast enough for me. It's too cold out there. Are you ready to go?"

"Let's hit it before I change my mind," Nicki warned as she grabbed her water bottle and house keys before they both stepped out into the cold and headed to the gym.

After they hung up their coats in a shared locker, they walked upstairs and made their way to the ellipticals. After programming her machine, Sissy started to speak.

"Nicki, I'm proud of you. You have really kept up your end of the bargain."

"Bargain?"

"Yeah, remember our talk at the Sonic last year after you and Angela had that falling out in the restaurant?

"Oh that." She cringed as the memory of stuffing herself with a banana split to ease her pain resurfaced. "Well, I have a long way to go yet."

"Don't dismiss the progress you've made so far," Sissy scolded. "Just be glad that you made the first move to better your health."

"You have a point there. But I'll admit that sometimes it's easier to just stay at home and curl up on my couch with Turner Classic Movies and a bowl of popcorn. When I'm here, I sweat and tire out so easily. And I feel so uncomfortable being around all of these people, I feel as if they're staring at how large I am. It's like they're laughing at me, asking themselves, 'What's her fat butt doing in here?'"

"Stop that! Do you think gyms are for the young and beautiful, the slim and pretty? Do you think these machines are only for the people with shapely or muscular figures? I'll answer it for you, NO. They're for people who want to stay in shape, but more importantly they're for people like you and me who want to *get into* shape."

The buzzer sounded on the machines to let them know the session had ended. After gathering their towels and water bottles they moved over to the treadmills, programmed forty minutes on the clock and continued their workout.

"OK Sissy, I get what you're saying but you have a reason to get in shape, you have Robert."

"What? Girl, before there was a Robert, all I had was me, myself and I. When I talked to you and Angela about getting into shape, it was because I was tired of my belly fat being my best friend," she patted her abdomen for emphasis.

"That was my wake-up call to do something about my health. In addition, my work with dialysis patients every day added an extra sense of urgency. A lot of them are on treatment because of uncontrolled hypertension, others because of issues with diabetes and still others because of some type of family history. There is always some underlying reason that causes these people to be on dialysis – and obesity is often a contributing factor.

"Wow, I never knew that," Nicki's voice revealed surprise.

Sissy continued. "Every morning I try to remember to thank God for my health, for making me the caregiver and not the receiver. In healthcare it's ironic that we are supposed to be helping people learn the importance of good health, and yet *we*, the nurses, doctors and other members of the field, are obese or smokers or on some type of medication for one aliment or another."

"You are really passionate about this aren't you?"

"Sorry Nicki, I didn't mean to preach, but to answer your question, yes, this means a lot to me. It's just that I love you so much and I want the best for you. You really deserve to be happy. I'm glad you asked me to join you this evening."

"Thanks Sissy, I love you too. I guess I need to work on my mental health, you know, more positive thinking. When you've been fat for so long, you become comfortable with it and learn to hide from the world."

"Well no more hiding, chick. It's time for you to break out of your shell!" Sissy chuckled. "Hey just think, in a few months we'll be boarding a plane for Heathrow Airport in London and after a couple of days we'll head to France. I'm so excited! I've picked up a language book at the library to study some common phrases in French."

"Me too! I figured since I'll be over there for a while, I might as well learn the language, or at least enough to ask for a glass of water and how to find the bathroom."

"What do you mean?" Sissy looked at her friend.

"Oh, I forgot to mention that my boss asked me to help him with an acquisition that our company is making. He's flying to Paris to personally handle the contract and, well, he asked that I join him."

"Nicki, get out of here! So you're staying over in Paris?"

"Just for a week or two, after I finish my vacation with you guys. I couldn't believe he chose me."

"Well Nicki, your hard work at that office has paid off. Congratulations. I should pop you upside your head for not mentioning this sooner!"

They completed their exercise and stepped off the machines. After patting away at the sweat on their faces and necks they headed towards the mats to stretch.

"I spoke to my brother last week. He said he can't wait to meet you and Angela."

"Did you tell him to be prepared for Ms. Thang?"

"Girl no! Angela is like a top secret weapon. You don't want anyone to know about it until you have to use it." They laughed while giving each other a fist bump and then took to the mats to cool down and relax.

—∞—

Nicki sat at one of the nearby picnic tables. The warm weather enticed people to dine outside. She pulled out her journal between bites of her sandwich and began to write.

Spring has finally arrived and with it, the budding of tulips along the Kansas City, Missouri boulevards. Occasionally winter threatens with whispers of cold air but Mother Nature pushes it away and in its place she sends tepid winds to welcome the new life, the budding of flowers and leaves all around.

I'm feeling a little philosophical today which is so unlike me. Maybe it's the thought that in a few months, we, Angela, Sissy and I, will be on our way to London then Paris. My passport arrived last week making the whole event so real. I wouldn't tell the girls but I shopped for a couple of pairs of slacks and a nice dress shirt for the trip. It's been awhile since I purchased anything new. I never had a need to, plus I hate trying on clothes while looking for things to cover my butt or to tug over my fleshy rolls. MAC make-up will take care of my face but the rest...Now that I will be representing my company in France; I want to look my best. I must not fail my boss or myself.

Angela parked the car on the back end of the company parking lot, the area with all the shade. The day had been both productive and tiring. She decided to take a break from the office and eat her lunch in the car away from clients, agendas, and office politics. Before starting on her roast beef sandwich with all the fixings, she reached for her journal in the passenger seat. As of late she'd begun to get into the spirit of jotting down a few notes when she had a spare minute.

I can't believe that it's already July and the Fourth is only a couple of days away, and after that - three more months and we'll be in Europe! I've tried to do some walking, at least thirty minutes three days a week, but it's so boring. I think I'll buy one of those music clip things to break up the monotony, otherwise I'll just step in front of a car and end it all. On a more positive note, I had one of my rare meetings with Paul not too long ago and told him about the upcoming trip. It turns out that he studied architecture in France for a couple of years and loved it. When he said something about Paris being "architecturally coherent" he immediately lost me, but that's alright, it gave me a chance to stare into those big dark eyes for 15 minutes. He's supposed to send me a list of must see buildings in Paris – humpf, the only must see buildings I'm visiting are the ones where I can buy Dior, Channel, and Louis Vuitton. But who knows, if he keeps popping up in my dreams like he did last night, I just might have to develop a new found interest in architecture...argh!

School supplies have filled the shelves with special 'Back to School' displays at Walmart, Kmart, Target and numerous grocery and drug stores to signal the return of fall. The summer season is coming to an end as parents rejoice at the fact that the children will return to school once again. Labor Day beckons the last hurrah as college dorms prepare to welcome its first year residents. It's the beginning of the end in so many ways. I hate to see the season disappear. It seems so short, not long enough before the leaves begin to change colors. In a few weeks the girls and I will be in London visiting William and then to Paris. I'm so glad that I have been hitting the gym five days a week. My weight loss has slowed down and that bothers me but as I stress to Nicki all the time, keep on pushin' on.

I'm really enjoying my time with Robert. Lately our schedules have been crazy but we try to squeeze in time together when we can. He's such a sweetheart and very supportive regarding my weight loss. I cringe when he touches my fat rolls but he doesn't complain. My embarrassment arises when I think of how shapely his former girlfriend, Candice looks compared to me.

Sissy closed her journal as the waitress approached the table with her lunch. She quietly said a blessing not only for her food but for her day off from the job. After her meal, Sissy planned to shop for a good pair of walking shoes for the trip.

thirty one

Sissy dashed through the doors of the Price Chopper grocery store and down the frozen food aisle. Grateful that she arrived before the after work crowd, she grabbed a few frozen meals that she could use for lunch for the next couple of days. Just as she turned the corner in the direction of the fruits and veggie aisle, she nearly collided with a woman in front of her.

"Oh, I'm sorry about that," she said. When she looked at the figure that stared back, her stomach tightened.

"Well I guess you need to slow down before you get a ticket," Candice joked. "Hello, again."

"Hi." Sissy stepped back to allow the woman to pass.

"You may want to find something nice and hot for dinner because Robert really enjoyed his grilled duck at the Classic Cup Café when we dined last week. Besides, he doesn't like frozen meals."

"For your information, this is my lunch Candice."

"Well, I hope things work out between you two. He's such a delicious little thing. Ciao baby."

She watched as the 5'5" figure in a pair of size 4 skinny jeans switched off.

thirty two

"OK, Mrs. Mackie, I'll see you on Tuesday at ten. Derick Williams and I will be out with the final plans for you and your husband's approval." Angela waved goodbye to the stout, thirty year old brunette that stood outside the thick, oak wood door.

She climbed into her car and started the ignition, fussing aloud, "It must be nice to have daddy's money to pay for baby girl's new home. 'Daddy said this and daddy said that'," Angela mocked the girl's southern drawl.

She put the car in reverse, turning the vehicle around as she continued her banter. "I should try to get with one of 'daddy's' handsome sons," she laughed after thinking of the family portrait that hung over the fireplace of the twenty room mansion she'd just left. Two of the men worked at the family brokerage firm while the other two were established lawyers, one for the father's company and the eldest with a local respected law firm.

"In fact, 'daddy' would have a conniption fit if one of his boys walked in with this fine piece of chocolate, dressed in something form fitting and sexy while hanging off his son's arm." Angela laughed at the thought then turned up the radio as the tune, "*Ice Ice Baby*" by Vanilla Ice blared through the speakers while she drove down the half mile driveway.

Before she exited the wrought iron gates, something rose up inside her and broke free.

"I hate you Cody!" she screamed before jerking the wheel to the right and stopping in front of a tree, placing the car into park. Her fists pounded the steering wheel as tears streamed down her face.

"We were supposed to be together, a fine home, money and a travel lifestyle. Why did you *do* this to me? I loved you Cody."

She wept with such force that she felt her heart pound in her chest. Her head fell forward on the steering wheel. It had finally happened. All the pain she didn't want her friends to see spilled out, exposing Angela to the raw emotions that she could no longer laugh or joke about.

Twenty minutes had passed before she finally raised her head and looked around to get her bearings. She was spent, but felt an odd sense of renewal. Angela took a deep breath and released it while reaching for her purse, removing her compact.

A tear stained face with smudged mascara stared back. "Enough," she said. "It's time to move on."

She repaired her make-up, sat erect in the driver's seat, put the car into gear and moved forward down the road and with her life.

Angela circled the lot at Red Robin twice before she noticed a car backing out of its space. She nabbed it quickly and then entered the restaurant.

"Well, it's about time you showed up," Nicki said after swallowing her ginger ale.

"Did you not get my text? I said I was stuck in traffic and would be here as soon as I could."

"Look you two," Sissy interrupted. "This is not The Fight of the Century, and you," she pointed at Nicki, "are not Muhammad Ali. And you," this time looking in Angela's direction, "are not Joe Frazier." She took a deep breath and let it out. The waitress returned to the table and took the women's orders then turned and walked away. Sissy continued. "What's wrong Ms. Thang?"

"Oh, nothing that a half a million dollars couldn't resolve," she sighed and flipped the long locks of hair over her shoulder. "Look, don't mind me. I just spent an hour and half with the 'almost young and restless'."

"Let's regroup," Sissy said. "I spoke to William recently to confirm our plans. Unfortunately, he lives in a studio apartment but he made arrangements for us to stay in a hostel while we're visiting in London."

"That was nice of him," Angela commented sarcastically.

"What's a hostel?"

"It's like renting a bunk bed in a dormitory with a shared bathroom. Sometimes they may throw in the lounge and kitchen if you're lucky. People on a tight budget use them," Angela said smugly.

The food arrived; Sissy and Nicki started on their Cajun turkey burgers wrapped in lettuce while Angela dove into her Whiskey River BBQ burger. They shared a basket of fries and the restaurant's signature Tower of Onion Rings.

"Anyway," Sissy began after swallowing a bite of her food, "his boss was nice enough to give him a couple of days of vacation when he found out I was coming to town. My brother will be our chauffer and tour guide during our visit so we won't have to spend money on cabs or the London Underground. He offered to drop us off at the airport the day we depart for Paris."

"That's a blessing," Nicki said between bites of her onion ring.

"But here's the best part, I booked our rooms in Paris! It's the Best Western Left Bank Saint Germain. They have a ninety-one percent approval rating on the Trip Advisor website."

"Wow," Angela exclaimed, "that makes this whole thing so...real."

"Yeah," Nicki added, "before, it was just something on paper that we talked about all the time. Now..."

"In four weeks we'll be flying the blue skies to our dream vacation." Sissy let out a squeal causing her friends to laugh aloud.

Once they settled down, Angela asked, "So is this fabulous place close to anything or do we have to climb through mountain passes and cross cold streams to get to everything?"

"Girl, you are so silly," Nicki laughed after picturing herself with hiking gear and a full pack strapped to her backside while yodeling.

"Nope, we're golden. The hotel is a ten minute walk from Notre Dame Cathedral and the Sainte Chapelle. To get to the Louvre and other attractions, shops and restaurants on the Right Bank will take us fifteen minutes."

"Sounds like we'll get a lot of exercise," Nicki said. "And don't you say a word Angela."

"I won't," she huffed.

"What's wrong with you two? We're about to spend a week in Europe. Please get whatever anger issues you may have under control. *I* plan to enjoy myself in *La Ville Lumière.*"

"What did you say?" Nicki asked.

"I said I plan to enjoy myself in the City of Light. According to one theory, Paris was one of the first cities to make extensive use of gas lamps to light their streets, thus earning them the nickname of 'The City of Light'."

"Oh, somebody's been doing a little research. Go on with your bad self," Angela said jokingly.

"Angela," Nicki started, "I forgot to mention, when you and Sissy return to Kansas I won't be joining you."

"What?"

She went on to explain the events of the merger.

"Some people get all the lucky breaks. Maybe I should stay and be your chaperon," Angela offered with a laugh.

"Ah, no thanks. I think I can handle this one just fine."

"Whatever." Angela pretended to be miffed. "When those Parisian men get a look at me they'll think I'm Josephine Baker, back from the dead."

"So you're planning to perform, *La Folie du Jour?*" Sissy questioned.

"What's that?"

"It was the dance that propelled Josephine Baker to stardom and made her one of the highest paid performers in France. She wore a skirt that was made of little more than sixteen bananas."

"That's all? No bra, no top?"

"I said sixteen bananas."

"Well, I guess I won't be doing *that* dance because these tatas need some steel beams to hold them up." All three women broke out in wild laughter.

"I've heard it all," Sissy snickered trying to get her breathing under control. "I'm going home." She grabbed her purse after stuffing a few bills into the folder that held her receipt. Angela and Nicki picked up their credit cards and joined their friend as she headed out the door.

thirty three

Winter's teeth took a bite out of Sissy's skin when she opened the front door and stepped outside. Instinctively she clutched her rust colored wool coat tighter while struggling with the hard shell suitcase, finally pulling it past the door. After loading it into the car she ran back into the house to warm her hands.

Sissy dropped her coat across the bannister and headed for the kitchen. While the water for her hot chocolate boiled, she thought of the night before and how the girls had teased her during the *Bon voyage* party that was held in her living room.

"What the heck is all this stuff?" Angela asked while pointing at the brightly colored suitcase.

"It's a fun, comic strip montage of New York City, the people and their famous sites. So what if it's kind of bright? I like it." Sissy placed a stack of clothes then her toiletries inside the open case. She heard the girls snicker and continued with her defense.

"Laugh all you want, at least I'll be able to spot my crazy looking luggage as it comes down the ramp onto the airline carousel a lot faster than your 'look alike' black bag Angela. And Nicki, don't think you're getting away from my wrath."

"What did I say?" she exclaimed.

"You were laughing right along with Cruella de Vil."

"Sissy, that wasn't me." Nicki tried, unsuccessfully, not to snicker.

"That's OK. I understand that you can't do any better than that old, navy blue, plain Jane suitcase. I guess you better find some Christmas ribbons or fancy duct tape to place on the handles so you can locate it. Better yet, maybe you should make a sign that reads, 'Hey you! I'm over here'."

Angela snorted and choked on the Chardonnay she had just swallowed. Nicki patted the corners of her eyes as tears spilled over from so much laughter.

Sissy shook her head. "When you two clowns finally get yourselves together, eat some more of that food I put out for you. Those meat and cheese trays are not cheap," she said as she continued to pack. The bon voyage party was in full swing as *Dodsworth*, a 1930s travel-inspired movie began on the flat screen television. Just as they settled down with their plates piled with food, they heard the doorbell.

"I'll get it," Nicki sang out.

She pushed her plate away while scrambling to her feet then headed to the hallway. She opened the main door and peered over the shoulder of a stocky framed man who stood on the other side of the screen, and noticed the words, "Edible Arrangements" plastered on the vibrantly colored delivery van. He held up an adorable, medium sized red bowl with a clever 'bouquet' of pineapples shaped as flowers, chocolate dipped strawberries and paper flags of different nations that could be seen through the cellophane.

She pushed the door open while he stared at her before asking, "Are you Ms. Bakersfield?"

"No, just a minute. Hey, Sissy!"

"Yeah, what is—," Sissy gasped as she stared at the beautiful bouquet. After signing for the gift she placed it on the coffee table in the living room, tore away the wrapping, removed the card inside, and read the message aloud:

Bon appetit! Have fun tonight with your girls! Sweet dreams, and I'll see you in the morning. Robert.

Angela and Nicki made kissing noises while scrunching up their faces. She ignored them, pulled out a chocolate covered strawberry, and before popping it into her mouth said in a mocking tone, "Don't hate me because I'm beautiful."

"Whatever," Nicki began, "so what's the deal between you and Robert?"

"What do you mean?" Sissy asked while wiping strawberry juice from her fingertips."

"I mean, you two have been seeing each other for a while. Are you serious about him or is he just a fill-in?"

"A fill-in?" she frowned.

"Yeah," Angela interjected. "Just a boy toy until what you really want comes along. After all, you're beginning to shape up and I must admit you're going to be very hot when it's all said and done."

"What's gotten into you two? Why this sudden interest in my love life?"

"Because we like Robert." Nicki said while moving toward the couch and having a seat. "Look at how considerate he is," she continued while pointing to the fruit bouquet."

"Yeah, he's nice and all that but it's still early in the game. He may have a change of heart."

"I don't think so," Angela remarked while plucking a flower shaped pineapple from its stem.

Sissy felt uneasy and quickly changed the subject.

"Enough about me. I need to finish packing. Oh, here's that part in the movie when the wife flirts with that young guy."

The thought of being tied down in a relationship felt confining and was the last thing she wanted to discuss at that moment.

"How odd that now, as I'm beginning to get into shape and get noticed by other men, I don't want to be in a relationship. The one thing I've always longed for is coming true — so why am I acting like a mad woman trying to run away from it? Besides, after my little bout with Candice, how much of a 'sure thing' is Robert, anyway?

"OK, it's time for 'Truth or Dare'," Angela yelled while pausing the movie.

"Truth or what?" Nicki asked.

"Yeah, we've got to find out much weight we all lost. Remember, this trip *is* supposed to be a reward for having lost weight."

"Oh, brother. OK, I'll start," Sissy said. "I've lost eighteen pounds and have dropped one dress size, but I've plateaued, and I'm kind of disgusted."

"Well, I've lost twenty pounds, and I've been on a plateau since Savannah, so don't feel bad," Nicki said.

"Yeah, but don't forget, because of all the extra workouts you've been doing you've dropped two dress sizes instead of one, like me."

"Oh, I didn't think of it like that," Nicki conceded.

"And Missy, what about you?" Sissy asked while turning towards Angela.

"Well, don't forget you two had a head start, and don't forget I'm still mending from a broken heart, and oh yeah, don't forget my surgery…"

"Girl, stop! How much did you lose?" Sissy interrupted.

"Well, I've lost eight pounds." Angela whispered.

"Sorry, I can't hear you," Nicki yelled.

"I SAID eight pounds."

"Oh, congratulations Angela," Nicki and Sissy snickered.

Angela picked up a pillow and hurled it at her friends, as they all broke out in laughter.

<hr />

The kettle's loud squeal caught her attention and Sissy focused on the task at hand. She prepared a cup of hot chocolate, scrambled an egg, and toasted two slices of sourdough bread. Just as she was about to take a bite, she heard a knock on the door followed by the high shrill of Angela's voice.

"What is this madness that's going on outside? Who told old man winter to show up?"

"I'm in the kitchen," Sissy called out.

Angela followed her friend's voice into the next room then plopped down in a chair. "Good morning bright eyes." She dropped her purse on the table then reached for a slice of toast, slathered with butter and apple jelly.

"Excuse you," Sissy said and smacked Angela's hand.

"I'm company," she pouted.

"In this house, it's every man for himself. By the way, where's baby girl?"

"Here I am," Nicki answered while stepping into the kitchen. She walked over and hugged her friend before taking a seat.

"Well aren't you looking cute in your outfit?" Sissy said while admiring the indigo blue, knit tunic with matching trouser length pants. She wore a pair of light blue sneakers.

"Thanks!" Nicki walked over to the cabinet for a bowl. "I didn't have a chance to eat before Angela showed up. Do you mind?"

"Be my guest," Sissy said as she finished her breakfast. "You may want to bag up some of that fruit from last night and stash a few granola bars in your carry-on bag because they only serve peanuts or pretzels on most flights, if you're lucky. The sandwiches are usually overpriced and of questionable taste."

"That's right," Angela said in the middle of eating her egg and cheese sandwich. The two women smiled at their friend.

"Hey girls, I'm going to run upstairs to grab a few last minute items," Sissy said hurrying out of the kitchen.

Fifteen minutes later she returned, finding Nicki at the sink while Angela, pencil in hand, outlined her lips using the mirrored reflection from the toaster. She held a tube of Warm Raisin lipstick between her fingers. Sissy shook her head, amazed at her friend's ingenuity whenever beauty was concerned.

"OK ladies, are we ready to go?"

"Where's Mr. Tall, dark and handsome? Angela asked while applying her lipstick.

"He'll be here."

"I finished the dishes and put them away," Nicki mentioned while wringing out the dish towel.

"Thanks." Sissy walked across the room, gave her friend a hug then pulled out a box of zip lock storage bags from the cabinet. As she continued chatting with Nicki, she filled one with raisins and almonds and another with Welches fruit snacks and granola bars.

After shooting a quick glance at her friends, Angela turned aside, grabbed her purse, and furtively pulled out her cell phone. A brief frown crossed her face as she gazed at the empty screen and shoved the phone back in the bag. Looking up, she caught Nicki leaning against the sink staring at her quizzically, Angela played it off and shouted, "Hey Sissy, where's my goodie bag?"

"In the goodie cabinet," Sissy joked. "I told both of you yesterday, you're not company in this house. So if you want something to eat, you better get your hips over here because I'm not sharing."

"Oh no you didn't," Angela barked.

Sissy shook her head and walked out, leaving the two women to rummage the cabinets like squirrels storing up nuts for the winter. She placed her food in the backpack and secured the flap just as the doorbell chimed.

"Man, it's no joke out there. It must be twenty degrees," Robert exclaimed, stepping through the door that Sissy held open.

He kissed her gently. "So how's my pretty lady?"

"Fine now that I've seen you." She kissed him back.

"I bet you say that to all the handsome men that come into your house," he joked.

"You know, you're right. I told Denzel that very thing last night."

"What?" his voice a little higher than normal. Without warning, he picked her up, slinging her over his right shoulder in one fell swoop.

"Robert put me down!" she squealed.

"First you have to apologize." He slapped her backside.

"Ouch! Robert, stop!"

"What's all this noise out here," Nicki shouted before stepping into the hallway. Angela followed while holding her goodie bag.

"Hello ladies," he said while setting Sissy on her feet.

"It's a shame," Angela began, "that you have to resort to such caveman antics to get your woman under control."

"A man's got to do what a man's got to do with these wild females."

"He's jealous." Sissy repeated her Denzel comment to them.

"Humpf," Robert gave his coat lapels a tug. "Denzel doesn't have a thing on me."

"That's right," Angela went to his defense and slipped her hand through his right arm.

"She doesn't understand you Robert," Nicki said in sad and consoling voice. "In fact how could she? Why don't you and I go have a nice cup of coffee?" Nicki took up his other arm and the girls walked him into the kitchen leaving Sissy standing with her hands on her full hips, alone, in the hallway.

"Don't believe a word he says," Sissy called out.

She walked to the living room to do a last minute check before heading to the airport. Just as she was about to return to the hallway, she turned, looked back, and noticed the miniature flags and notecard on the coffee table. Her pulse quickened as she recalled last night's conversation.

"I'm not ready to settle down with one man," she protested in a low voice. "I have too many people to meet, places to see and ...Candice..."

Before she could finish, Angela called out. "We better hit the road gang so we're not late."

Sissy let out a sigh and joined her friends as they made their way to the front door.

thirty four

The forty-five minute drive to the airport looped past The Legends Outlet mall, the Kansas Speedway, and beyond that, acres of farmland.

Nicki and Angela sat in the backseat of the car absorbed in thought while Robert drove and Sissy relaxed and enjoyed the view. Every so often Robert reached for Sissy's hand as the car coasted down the highway.

Nicki pulled out her journal and scribbled,

I hope that I can get through this trip without embarrassing myself, I don't want to be the fat girl that ruins it for everyone else. Now that I have the extension regarding the job, I'll continue to walk for exercise while I get to know Paris on a more intimate level. Who knows, maybe I'll finally be able to deal with my guilt, that secret that's held me back for so long. So many lies, so many pounds would just fall away."

She closed the book and stuffed it into her purse.

Angela stared out the passenger window. The landscape was a blur as she recalled her meltdown a few days ago. This trip would put distance between the last vestiges of her broken heart. She hated feeling like a jilted lover who couldn't move on. What happened to the old Angela; the flirty, sassy chick that could turn a man's head? She prayed that Paris would bring her back to her senses.

Sissy thought of William and the need to connect to her brother once more. She missed him so much but most of all she needed the

186 | Lila Johnson

time away from Robert. The fear of falling into a 'routine' with him made her nervous. Yes he was kind, respectful and showed a deep affection for her, but *now* she had so many doubts about this relationship. Her escape to London and Paris could come none too soon. She needed space, and lots of it.

When they were fifteen minutes from the airport, Robert spoke, breaking into her thoughts.

"Make sure to call me as soon as you clear customs so that I'll know you made it safely."

"I rented a special cell phone for this trip so I wouldn't have any problems with overseas calls. Thanks again for driving us to the airport. This will save us a lot of money in parking fees."

"It's no problem baby. Now you'll have a little more cash to spend in Paris." He brought her left hand to his mouth and kissed her palm twice before releasing it. "Don't worry about your mail, I'll pick it up and check on your place while you're away. I wish I could hang out with you and your buddies at the airport but I have to get back to the job site."

"I understand." She gave his arm a squeeze then turned her gaze back to the road.

"Hey Robert," Nicki called out. "Thanks for being so good to our friend."

"Yeah," Angela interrupted, "because if you weren't, I'd have to put a hurting on you."

"A what?

"I'd have to kick your …"

"Angela!" I think he got the picture," Sissy called out.

Robert laughed while looking in the rearview mirror at both women. "Ladies, I wouldn't do anything to hurt your friend, at least not on purpose."

"That's good to know," Sissy said then leaned over to kiss his cheek. As they drove down the boulevard leading to the airport, all eyes looked for the directional signs that led to the United Airlines drop-off.

Kansas City International Airport was nothing like JFK, LAX or Chicago O'Hare, but it held its own in servicing all the major airlines, domestic and international, and it was the best in terms of accessibility.

As he approached the terminal, the women opened their purses and checked their wallets for identification, passports and travel itineraries. Angela covertly pulled out her cell phone then sighed deeply, still holding the phone in her hand.

"What's wrong?" Nicki whispered? "This is the umpteenth time you've checked that thing since we left Sissy's place."

"Don't worry about it," Angela answered briskly, turning her face toward the window.

Sissy touched her chest briefly, a feeling of tightness jolting her. Maybe the excitement of seeing her brother triggered it or could it have been the thought of leaving Robert, even for a little while? She realized that the departure wasn't forever, but still...

Robert pulled to the curb and turned on the car's flashers, then jumped out and headed to the trunk of the car followed by Angela and Nicki. As he removed the suitcases, they quickly grabbed bags, knowing that security would soon drive by to announce the time limitation regarding parking. Each gave him a hug then entered the airport through the double glass doors.

Robert handed Sissy her suitcase and gazed gently in her eyes, "Now remember what I told you. Be safe and have fun." His voice was full of emotion. He gathered Sissy in his arms and kissed her deeply, with all the passion he could safely display without attracting too much attention. Robert pulled away first, still staring into her eyes.

"I'll miss you. Hurry back to me."

"I will," she said then kissed him once more.

Just then, a police car cruised by. "Fifteen minutes for loading and unloading," he announced on his loud speaker. "Do not leave cars unattended."

"You'd better go sweetie," Sissy said after glancing at the police car. They kissed for the last time then he placed a bright yellow tote bag on her shoulder. Once she stepped onto the sidewalk, she paused to wave goodbye and watched as he merged into the airport traffic, disappearing from her view. Sissy grabbed the handle of her suitcase and walked through the parted doors to join her friends.

"The next time I go to an airport," Angela huffed after grabbing her purse, shoes and carry-on while hobbling over to the first available seat, "I'm just going to come in my panties and bra and dress afterward."

"Tell me about it," Nicki said as she settled in a nearby chair. Her shoes were half on, half off while she dragged the tote bag behind her. "I feel so...violated."

Sissy joined them and plopped down beside Angela. "Someone hand me a cigarette." The two women looked at her as though she had lost her mind. "I just made love to an X-ray machine and I need to relax." They all broke out in fits of laughter so loud that people walking by glanced in their direction.

They arrived in the United Airlines waiting area, found three available seats and settled down for the forty minute wait. Sissy rechecked her purse and backpack once more.

"Better to be over cautious than surprised later, she said."

Nicki followed suit, while Angela indulged in one more disappointing look at her cell phone. As boarding time approached, the excitement was palpable when the three women heard the crackle of the overhead intercom come to life.

"Ladies and gentlemen," the agent began, "we will begin boarding in a few minutes. When we start, we will call for all first class and business travelers. Our next passengers to board early will be all military personnel and finally those with disabilities or with small children. We will announce coach seating by groups. Please, do not attempt to board before your group is called. This is a full flight and we ask that everyone cooperate so that we can depart on time."

Nicki yelped.

Angela jumped and looked around. "You nut, was that you that made that crazy noise?"

"We're on our way to London!" she beamed. The two women laughed and shook their heads.

"I hate to be the bearer of bad tidings Nicki, but we fly to Washington, D.C. first, then to London," Sissy corrected her.

"Either way, we are still going to London!"

Soon their group was called and the three moved into line, boarding pass in hand.

"Hey Nicki, now that we're on our way, I've appointed myself as your chaperone the whole time we're over there," Angela said.

"I don't think so Ms. Know It All. I plan to see Big Ben, the Crown Jewels, have tea and crumpets. Oh, and I want to take a peek at the new prince, Baby George. Then it's off to Paris."

"Now *that's* my playground," Angela interjected. "The shops, the men, the..."

"Ladies, ladies," Sissy called out. "Could we get our hips into our seats first and worry about the other stuff later."

They finally made their way through first class and then into 'Hell's Kitchen' as Angela called the coach section. After they put away their carry-on luggage, Sissy settled near the window while Nicki took the aisle seat. Angela reluctantly sat across from them, next to an impish looking man who had just sneezed inside the yellow mask he was wearing.

Sissy had forgotten that she was still holding her boarding pass and reached for her backpack to put it away. It was one of the mementos that she would add to her journal later. As she unzipped the pack, she remembered the bright yellow tote bag that Robert had placed on her shoulder right before she'd entered the airport. After the security check, she'd inadvertently stuffed it into the backpack. She pulled out the tote, reached inside, and removed a small, brightly wrapped item with the words SURPRISE written in bold letters on the paper.

"What's that?" Angela asked, pointing to the package.

"I don't know, I just found it."

Sissy pushed the pack under the seat in front of her as she watched the stewardess make her way down the aisle. She ripped the paper with childlike abandon, giggling at the gift she held in her hand. Angela shook her head when Sissy held up a gnome, dressed in a bright red hat, dark blue coat and brown pants. She pulled out a small green passport and read aloud a detailed history of the gnome's life starting with his full name and birthplace.

"He reminds me of that Travelocity roaming gnome in the television commercials," Nicki snickered. "I guess we have a stowaway."

Sissy read the card that was tucked into the tote, "Since I can't come with you, I'm sending my proxy to keep an eye on you, bon voyage!"

The three women laughed, and then took turns snapping pictures of each other while holding the little figure in their hands posed near their faces. "I think Robert likes you," Angela teased while handing the gnome back to her friend.

"Yeah...," she mumbled while placing the gift back into the box that was laying on her lap.

Angela looked at the picture of the gnome on her cell phone and grinned, she was about to click off when a text message popped up on the screen:

"Hey Angela, here's that list of buildings I promised to send you: *chose promise, chose due*, or as we'd say in English, what's promised is due. And now, I want YOU to promise to give me a full report when you get back – Bon voyage! Paul."

Angela looked up from the phone and was surprised to see Nicki and Sissy staring at her.

"Girl, I've been calling your name for the last five seconds," Sissy chided.

"Yeah, and what's that little smile on your face all about?" Nicki teased.

"*Chose promise, chose due,*" Angela answered mysteriously using her best fake French accent.

"Translation, please, Ms. Multilingual," Sissy huffed.

The jet's engines revved louder as the overhead television screens came to life and a voice from the intercom filled the cabin.

"That'll have to wait girls," Angela laughed as she slipped the cell phone in her purse, and whispered, "Paul...? Paris...? Maybe Paul..."

"Ladies and gentlemen, welcome aboard United 4618 in route to Washington, DC. If you realize you are on the wrong flight, I would advise you to jump off now while there's still time."

The cabin roared to life with laughter.

"This is your captain, James Royce along with my co-pilot Matthew Hanes. Your cabin stewardesses are Melanie, Debra and Sara. We ask that all electronic devices are turned off and all carry-on items are stowed away in the overhead bins or under the seats in front of you. As we prepare for takeoff please make sure that your seatbelts are secure. We will show a short safety video as we taxi into position. Thank you for flying with us and we hope you enjoy your flight."

The three women held hands and prayed silently. Once they'd finished they opened their eyes and smiled.

"First stop, Washington, then London," Sissy said. "Thanks for taking this journey with me. I can think of no finer companions than my two sisters."

"Just like the Three Musketeers," Angela chuckled.

"All for one and one for all," Nicki smiled.

The plane taxied down the tarmac gaining speed until its nose pointed upward into the silent, blue afternoon sky. Sissy pulled a new red, leather journal from her backpack and jotted her first entry:

"This is our journey, Angela, Nicki and I. We're about to experience new adventures, grow as friends, and learn things about one another that we've never shared before. May we put aside our fears and open our hearts to the lessons that life places before us. Make us strong, keep us well, and may laughter follow us wherever we may go. In the name of Jesus. Amen."

11194357R00108

Made in the USA
Monee, IL
08 September 2019